Duplin County, NC
AFRICAN AMERICAN EXPERIENCE

Book Dedication

Glorious Chasten Boykins

James and Helen Dobson McGowan

This book is dedicated to these individuals for their major contributions of African American History in Duplin County, North Carolina. Your unselfish dedication and commitment to preserve African American history will never go unnoticed.

Everyone that reads this book will know for many years to come that you all have given your time and resources to help make this make this book a success!

You guys are the best and I will never forgot your labor of love!

Desi L. Campbell

About The Author

Desi L. Campbell is a native of Washington, DC. He is a 1993 graduate of Johnson C. Smith University in Charlotte, North Carolina with a B.A. in Music Business. He also attended Savannah State University in Savannah, Georgia and Fayetteville State University in Fayetteville, North Carolina.

While at Johnson C. Smith, Desi participated in the band, concert choir and served as the President and Director of the R. W. Johnson Gospel Choir. He also founded the Friends Ensemble. During his time at Savannah State University, he was a member of the Achievers of Today and Tomorrow, Inc., The Savannah State University Concert Choir, and served as the president of the Wesleyan Gospel Choir.

Desi, a passionate community servant, was a member of the 100 Black Men of Savannah, the Savannah Mass Choir and founded the Perfecting Praise Chorale. In 2006, he pledged Phi Beta Sigma Fraternity, Inc. by way of the Tau Beta Sigma Chapter. Professionally, Desi served East Broad Street Elementary School as a technology instructor for nine years. During that time, he was honored to lead students who competed in the International Student Media Festival for several years. Those students were afforded the opportunity to travel to Anaheim, California and won 1st place for their media project. Campbell served on local, state and national committees for the International Student Media Festival. Always an advocate for youth, he established several youth programs in the community. Project HYPE. (Helping Younger People Excel), The Savannah State Music and Arts Summer Camp and the Perfecting the Arts Summer Academy, where he served as the Executive Director. Campbell and the Perfecting Praise Chorale of Savannah, GA were featured in the Savannah Music Festival Concert Series in 2005.

In Charlotte, Campbell founded the National Collegiate Music Conference in 1992 on the campus of Johnson C. Smith University. This conference served over 2000 high schools, colleges, and community groups from all over the United States. Campbell has recorded 4 albums with this group: We Are One, Possess the Land, Wait on the Lord, and Get Ready for the Outpour.

Currently residing in Harnett County, Desi has served on the Board of Directors of the Sandhills Family Heritage Association, the Harnett County Branch of the NAACP as treasurer, and the Harnett County African American Caucus. He is the Executive Director of the African American Heritage Center, Harnett County African American Heritage Festival, the Harnett County Juneteenth Festival, and owner of "Let's Print, LLC. in Lillington, NC. He is currently employed with Harnett County Schools as a Music Teacher and currently working on a certificate of completion in the Digital Media Program at Fayetteville Technical College.

Duplin County Slave Narrative
Lizzie Baker

I was born de las' year o' de surrender an' course I don't remember seein' any Yankee soldiers, but I knows a plenty my mother and father tole me. I have neuritis, an' have been unable to work any fer a year and fer seven years I couldn't do much.

My mother wus named Teeny McIntire and my father William McIntire. Mammy belonged to Bryant Newkirk in Duplin County. Pap belonged to someone else, I don't know who.

Dey said dey worked from light till dark, and pap said dey beat him so bad he run away a lot o' times. Dey said de paterollers come to whare dey wus havin' prayer meetin' and beat 'em.

Mammy said sometimes dey were fed well and others dey almost starved. Dey got biscuit once a week on Sunday. Dey said dey went to de white folks's church. Dey said de preachers tole 'em dey had to obey dere missus and marster. My mammy said she didn't go to no dances 'cause she wus crippled. Some o' de help, a colored woman, stole something when she wus hongry. She put it off on mother and missus made mother wear trousers for a year to punish her.

Mammy said dey gave de slaves on de plantation one day Christmas and dat New Years wus when dey sold 'em an' hired 'em out. All de slaves wus scared 'cause dey didn't know who would have to go off to be sold or to work in a strange place. Pap tole me 'bout livin' in de woods and 'bout dey ketchin' him. I 'member his owner's name den, it wus Stanley. He run away so bad dey sold him several times. Pap said one time dey caught him and nearly beat him to death, and jest as soon as he got well and got a good chance he ran away again.

Mammy said when de Yankees come through she wus 'fraid of 'em. De Yankees tole her not to be 'fraid of 'em. Dey say to her, 'Do dey treat you right', Mammy said 'Yes sir', 'cause ole missus wus standin' dere, an' she wus 'fraid not to say yes. Atter de war, de fust year atter de surrender dey moved to James Alderman's place in Duplin County and stayed dere till I wus a grown gal.

Den we moved to Goldsboro. Father wus a carpenter and he got a lot of dat work. Dat's what he done in Goldsboro. We come from Goldsboro to Raleigh and we have lived here every since. We moved here about de year o' de shake and my mother died right here in Raleigh de year o' de shake. Some of de things mother tole me 'bout slavery, has gone right out of my min'. Jes comes and goes.

I remember pap tellin' me' bout stretchin' vines acrost roads and paths to knock de patterollers off deir horses when dey were tryin' to ketch slaves. Pap and mammy tole me marster and missus did not 'low any of de slaves to have a book in deir house. Dat if dey caught a slave wid a book in deir house dey whupped 'em. Dey were keerful not to let 'em learn readin' and writin'.

Dey sold my sister Lucy and my brother Fred in slavery time, an' I have never seen 'em in my life. Mother would cry when she was tellin' me 'bout it. She never seen 'em anymore. I jes' couldn't bear to hear her tell it widout cryin'. Dey were carried to Richmond, an' sold by old marster when dey were chillun.

We tried to get some news of brother and sister. Mother kept 'quiring 'bout 'em as long as she lived and I have hoped dat I could hear from 'em. Dey are dead long ago I recons, and I guess dare aint no use ever expectin' to see 'em. Slavery wus bad and Mr. Lincoln did a good thing when he freed de niggers. I caint express my love for Roosevelt. He has saved so many lives. I think he has saved mine. I want to see him face to face. I purely love him and I feel I could do better to see him and tell him so face to face.

Source: Slave Narratives: a Folk History of Slavery in the United States From Interviews with Former Slaves, North Carolina Narratives, Vol. XI, Part 2. Vol. XI, Publ. 1941. The Federal Writer's Project, 1936-1938. Library of Congress. Contributed by Kim Paterson)

Enslaved
OF DUPLIN COUNTY

WILLS, DEEDS AND PROBRATE RECORDS

6

State of North Carolina }
Duplin County } 12 January 1805

To the Worshipfull Court of Pleas and Quarter
Sessions for the County aforesaid

We the subscribers being a committee appointed
at last court to divide the estate of William
[illegible] of said estate have proceeded as followeth

We have valued Negro Tony at ———— 250
                        Davy ———— 225
                        Isaac ———— 140
                        Bill ———— 115
                        Peter ———— 115
                        Cate ———— 115
                        Penny ———— 80
                        Flora ———— 60
                        Reuben ———— [illegible]

Total value of the Negro Estate £1145

Due from John McGowen Interest included } 67 – 16 – 11
till January term 1805

Due from William McGowen interest } 76 – 18 – 1
included till January term 1805

Due from Edward McGowen Interest } 6 – 15 – [?]
included   [January] term 1805

State of North Carolina } To the Worship-
Duplin County   } full Court of
Pleas and quarter sessions to it at October
term next. —

The Subscribers appointed last C[ourt]
the Estate of William McGowen
dec'd so as to ascertain George McGowen's
Share of said Estate have proceeded as
follows. —

		Ds Cts
We have valued Negroe Toney at		450 "
	Joe	375 "
	Bill	325
Cate & her child Shadrick	275
	Penny	250 "
	Bob	150
Total value of the Negroe Estate		$1825 "

Am't of monies due from the other
heirs viz. from John, William, Edward
& James McGowen, including Interest
till July Court 1809, as appears from
report of Committee to January term
1805. — | 24 "

The Manor Plantation | 750 "
Total value of the Estate — $2599
one half of which is George McGowens
share of said Estate — $1299-50

which he has Rec'd in Negroe property to his satisfaction — as an equavalent for his share in the land which is willed to his younger brother Alexander McGowen We have valued to him Negroes to make his share equal — with which he is Satisfied

Negroes Let off to George McGow

	Toney at	450
Cate & child Shade	—	275
	Bob —	150
	Abby —	325
	Dave —	175
	Bill —	325
his share of	both	1700
the monied part of the other Estates —		167 – 28
total amount of his share		1867 – 28

Negroes that Remain to Alexander

McGowen —	Nance & child Whitfield —	$410
	Joe —	375
	Penny —	250
		50
his share of the manor plantation — both		92 – 28
the monied part of the Estates —		$1867 – 28
total amt of his share		

all which is submitted

July 21 – 1809

J McIntyre
Jo Gillespie
Edw'd Pearsall

Let the bearer Bob pass to Mr Low
Savages & return this Evening
Sep[br] 12 - 1813   John McGowen

Ed Pearsall 2 - 24
W - Hurst 7 - 50
             5 - 70

B - Chasten 20 - —
James Raphel 7 - 24
M James 20 - —
A Morgan 7 - 50
J. Rutledge 20 - 45
D Pearsal 34 - 70
              153 41

McGowen Received $153-41 in Notes

                           cnts
Pearsol $42 - 50
S - Stanford   3 - 60
J - Grayham   4 - 40
A Dickson   65 - —
G James   19 - 41
R Dickson   1 - 60
C Lea   1 - 92
H Hunter   10 - 51
                        37
Hilden Wilson —
Th Molten   1 - 40
Jo Canady   2 - 95
R - McGowen 4 - 50
Joseph Mallard 1 - 01
                   204 37
                        50
McGowen Received $204 In notes
       199 " 87

State of N°Carolina   April 28th 1797

To the Worshipful Court of Pleas & Quarter
Sessions for the County of Duplin

Your Committee appointed to divide
the Estate of William McGowen deceased have
proceeded as follows (viz)

We have valued
Big Harry at	£150..0..0
Little Harry at	140..
Old Peter	80
Toney	155..
Valentine	100..
Davy	85..
Sam	70..
Joe	50..
Peter	25..
Bill	25
Kate	100
Mary sold for	80
2 Years Interest on the price of Mary	9..12
Total value of the Negroes	£1069..12
William McGowen's Law valued at	150..
Edward McGowen's ditto	45..
Robert McGowen's ditto	62..10..
The Manor Plantation subject to Mrs. McGowens Dower	100..
Value of the whole Estate	£1457..2..

one fifth part of which being the
two deceased childrens part of the Estate
              Amounting to £291..8..5
one ninth part of which is John McGowens   32..7..7
share of the deceased childrens Estate amounting to

The following is a list of the negros [slaves?]
belonging to the estate of Joseph McGown —
which came into the hands of his
admr. Jno. D. McGowen — (viz)

aged years

Fanney
Hagar Sr
Melvina 1 child
Mariett 2 children
Eliza 1 child
Ell[en?]
Hagar
[Narcissa?]
Flora
Fanny
Tom
Rubin
Tom Sr
Alfred
Alen
Joe
George
Alex[?]
Tom Jr
Ned
Hy
Clay
Ben
John

Jno. D. McGowen Admr.

To the Chairman of the County Court of
Duplin North Carolina

The undersigned a committee appointed at October Term of the County Court of Duplin 1851 to divide the Slaves belonging to the Estate of the late Joseph McGowen among John D McGowen Edward Pearsoll & wife Margaret Thomas Hall & wife Mary, Julia A McGowen Charles B & Alexander S McGowen & Joseph Price & Hannah McGowen beg leave to report that they met at the residence of the late Joseph McGowen and made the following division on the 11th December 1851 No.1 Including George, Flora, Ely to Charles B McGowen valued at $1650 Sixteen hundred and fifty dollars No.2 To Julia A McGowen Including Alex, Mary, Clay, Fanny valued at $1850 Eighteen hundred & fifty dollars No.3 To Alexander S McGowen Including Tom, Malvena & two children Ben & Joe valued at $1700 Seventeen hundred dollars No.4 To John D McGowen Including Allen, Hagar Eliza & child William valued at $1850 Eighteen hundred & fifty dollars No.5 To Mrs Hannah F McGowen Including Alfred, Harriet & two children Lucy & Martha Charlotte, Ellen, valued at $1900 Nineteen hundred dollars Two hundred and seventy five dollars allowed this lot for keeping two old women Hagar & Fanny No.6 To Joseph Price Including Ned, Hagar, Colvin valued at $1750 Seventeen hundred & fifty dollars No.7 To Edward Pearsoll & wife Margaret Including Henry Mary & child Emey, Tom, John valued at $1850 Eighteen hundred & fifty dollars

State of North Carolina
Duplin County } 12 January 1805

To the Worshipfull Court of Pleas & Quarter Sessions for the County aforesaid —

Your Committee appointed at last Court to divide the estate of George McGowen decd so as to ascertain Joseph McGowens share of said Estate have proceeded as follows —

We have valued Negroes Nancy at — £ 175 —
Hagar at — 150 —
Abby at — 115 —

Which makes the total amt of Negroes £ 440

It appears that the administrators of said Estate are indebted interest included till January term 1805 } 51 – 2 – 8

due from John McGowen interest included till January term 1805 } 19 – 9 – 9

Due from Edward McGowen interest included to January term 1805 } 10 – 9 – 4

Due from Robert McGowen interest included till January term 1805 } 47 – 18 – 10

Due from James McGowen Interest included till January term 1805 } 10 – 2 – –

Which makes the total amt of the Estate £ 579 – 2 – 7

one third part of which is Joseph McGowens Share of said Estate } 193 – " – 10

from which deduct his share of leaves a balance due the other children } 386 – 1 – 9

The other Negroes viz old Nanny Nell Hagar Nancy & Abbie were left as a common Stock to be divided hereafter among the younger Children (viz) James, Michael, Joseph, George & Alexander.

Edward McGowen then paid to William McGowen the Balance due him of thirty pounds nineteen & five pence, & gave his note to the Administrators for Eighteen pounds 1/2 which settles the Balance due by him the said Edward

It is further reported to your Committee that the said George McGowen was possessed of certain Lands in New Hanover County which we do not consider within our Jurisdiction

All which is Submitted &c. Tho Routledge
Joseph Dickson
Benj Kidder

State of North Carolina } 28th April 1794
Duplin County   }

To the Worshipful Court of Pleas and Quarter Sessions for the County aforesaid.

Your Committee appointed to divide the Estate of the late George McGowen deceased have proceeded as follows, viz.

1st We have valued Negro Nanny at . . . £80 . 0 . 0
     "   "   Hannah at . . . 140 . 0 . 0
     "   "   Tom . . . 145 . 0 . 0
     "   "   Harry . . . 120 . 0 . 0
     "   "   Nell . . . 100 . 0 . 0
     "   "   Nancy . . . 75 . 0 . 0
     "   "   Haty . . . 65 . 0 . 0
     "   "   Hagar . . . 65 . 0 . 0
     "   "   Abby . . . 40 . 0 . 0
                Total value of the Negro Estate £830 . 0 . 0

2d   There also appeared by the Administrators to be a Balance due the Estate as hereinafter } 53 . 1

Sale of Negros Continued   Page 9

Name of Slave	Name of Purchaser	$	cts
Woman Chloe & Boy Diamond	B N Williams	750	00
Girl Hanah	Bryant Newkirk	825	00
" Mary	Abram N Mathis	935	00
" Creasy	W W Wayne	790	00
Boy Jasper	" " do	1065	00
" Ben	Henry Mathis	1200	00
Woman Hanah & Children 3	Bryant Newkirk	1300	00
Boy Alfred	L A Merriman	1120	00
" Virgil	Timothy Newkirk	655	00
" Swan	Timothy Newkirk	1025	00
Hire until sale	W Wilkins	17	50

G P Powers Administrator

Returned to October Term AD 1858

In the name of God Amen.

I James Kenan of the County of Duplin and State of North Carolina, being of Sound mind and knowing that it is appointed for man to die, do make and ordain this my last Will and Testament, in manner and form following, that is to say.; First and principally I recommend my Soul to God that gave it, and my Body to the Earth to be buried in a Christian manner at the discretion of my Executors, hereafter named.

And as to such worldly Estate, as it hath pleased God to bless me with in this life, I give and dispose of in the following manner.

First, it is my Will that all my just Debts should be paid out of such part of my Estate, that my Executors may think prop.

Item. I give and bequeath to my beloved wife Sarah Kenan my Negro wench Easter, and all her Children.

Item. I give and bequeath to my son Daniel Love Kenan two yellow men Slaves, to wit, Aleck & Moses, to him and his Heirs for ever. with my Plantation and all my lands joining the same, and also all my other lands of every kind (Except my Executors should think pr.   approve of of the lightwood land to pay my Debts.) in that case I leave it to their discretion. And all the Remainder part I give to him and his Heirs for ever.

Item. I give and bequeath to my son Thomas Kenan my Negro Wench Colly and her Child Henry, also I will and bequeath to him (all

In the name of God Amen.

    I Hugh Pearsall being in feeble health, yet of sound & disposing mind & memory, do make & publish this as my last Will & Testament in manner & form following. to wit, first I commend my Soul to God, & my Body to its mother earth. — As to my worldly substance I dispose of it as follows. first, I give to my beloved Wife Margaret my Slaves Buck & Warsaw to her & her Heirs forever, and I lend her during her life time my Negro Girl Polly, also lend her till my oldest living Child comes to lawful age or marries my Negro Girl Anny; And I lend her during her life time all the cleared part of the Plantation whereon I now live, with the full priviledge of getting any Timber that may be needed for the benefit of the Plantation except the cutting of Turpentine Box Trees — I also give to my said Wife two Beds & furniture with all the rest of my Household & Kitchen furniture (not hereinafter mentioned) my Plantation & farming Tools, my Gig & harness, my Side Saddle & bridle, two of my Horses (her choice), four Cows & Calves, my Stock of ~~Hogs~~ Sheep & Geese, my Ox Cart & fifty dollars in Cash to her & her Heirs forever, it being distinctly understood & admitted by me in making the above bequest that my Wife is the legal owner her life time of Slaves Luke & Mary. —

    Next. I give to my two Sons James D. & William F. all my Lands on Bear Marsh which I purchased from William Rhodes & Bryan Sollis, to be divided equally between them when the oldest comes to lawful age, and one feather Bed & furniture each, to them & their Heirs forever —

    Next I give to my daughter Sarah A. the Lands lent to my Wife (after her decease) my Mahogany Tables, half dozen table & tea Spoons each, & one Bed & furniture to her & her Heirs

Pursuant to an order to us directed to ~~divide the~~ real & personal estate of Edward Pearsall Decd between the heirs John Pearsall & Thomas H. Wright in behalf of his Wife we have met and proceeded to business we have allotted to John Pearsall the following Negroes (to wit) March valued at three Hundred & fifty Dollars $350 Jack at three Hundred & seventy five Dollars $375 Claborne at three Hundred Dollars $300 and Lott at One Hundred & Twenty five Dollars $125 And we have given to Thomas H Wright in behalf of his Wife Sam valued at five Hundred & Twenty five Dollars $525 Sarah at Three Hundred & Seventy five Dollars $375 Alfred at Two Hundred & fifty Dollars $250 Making an equal Share And have proced to divide the Land begining at the mouth of the Mill branch and running up the said branch as it meanders to the back Line giving to John Pearsall all the Land on the North side of sd branch and all on the South side to Thomas H Wright

19

mentioned in the petition begs leave to submit the following report: After due advertisement I proceeded to sell the said slaves at the Court House in Kinmundville on the 29th of March (Tuesday of Court) when & where they were disposed of as follows, to wit:

    Barney to Mrs. Mary Newkirk at $2000.
    Nelly & child to W.W. Wayne   " $3650
    Ellen   J.A. Newkirk   " 1250
                        Total $6900.

Your Commr further reports that he considers the above as fair prices and that he secured the several amounts by notes with good sureties at 6 mos with int. from date.

                        Respectfully,
                        D.T. McMillan Commr.

Account of Sales Continued — page 8

Article	Name of Purchaser	$	cts
1 Cow & Yearling	William Usher	10	50
2 Heifers each $5.37½	Samuel Bradshaw	18	00
2 Steers each $4.00	William Usher	8	00
2 Steers each $4.50	J. G. Fussell	9	00
5 Hogs at $4.25	Timothy Newkirk	21	25
3 do	" do	11	50
1 Sow & 2 Pigs	" do	6	00
4 Shoats	" do	18	00
1 Mr. Harnes & Box	" do	"	12
7 Sheep each $1.15	J. T. Pope	8	05
1 Lamb	John Drew		60
1 Sheep	Timothy Newkirk	1	00
1 Mare	" do	50	00
1 Mule	William Brice	153	00
1 do grey	Wm. B. Mathis	69	00
The Whole growing crop	Timothy Newkirk		
1 Bee Hive	" do		52
Ox yoke & Steel yoke	" do		50

Sale of Negroes

Priscilla & girl Frances	B. R. Newkirk	625	00
Jack	" " do	800	00
Joe	" " do	1000	00
William	" " do	850	00
Eliza	" " do	1200	00
Priscilla Jr	" " do	1500	00
Jim	J. D. Larison	955	00

I Andrew Stokes of the County of Duplin and State of North Carolina being of Sound mind and memory but considering the uncertainty of my earthly existance do make and declare this my last will and testament in maner and form following that is to Say first that my executor hereafter named Sall provide for my body a desent burial Suitable to the wishes of my relative and friends and pay all funeral expences together with my just debts howsoever and to whom Soever owing out of the moneys that may first come into his hands as a part or parcel of my estate

Item I give and bequeath to my daughter Jain Stokes my negrow man Slave named Abrem two beds and furniture

Item I give and bequeath to my daughter Elizabeth Stoke my negrow woman Slave named Jeanah two beds and furniture

Item it is my will and desire that what property I may possess at the time of my death be Sold and the money be equally diveded between my two daughters Jain Stokes and Elizabeth Stokes

and lastly I do hereby constitute and appoint my trusty friend Joseph Stokes my lawful executor to all intents and purposes to execute this my last will and testament according to the true intent and meaning of the Same

and every part and clause thereof hereby revoking and declairing utterly void all other wills and testaments by me heretofore made in witness whereof I the Said Andrew Stokes do hereunto Set my hand and and Seal this 16th day of October AD 1837

Signed sealed published and declared by the said Andrew Stokes to be his last will and testament in presence of

Robert Stokes

Nancy + Stokes
his/her mark

Andrew Stokes {Seal}

State of North Carolina
Duplin County

To the Worshipful the Justices of the Court of Pleas and Quarter Sessions January Term 1854

Pursuant to your order appointing the undersigned a Committee to audit and settle the accounts of Wm W. Miller and Jas H. Hicks Exts of Richard Miller Deceased have had the same under consideration and ask leave to submit the following report

Amount of Vendue sales returned by the Exts including Interest to 1st January 1854	$1290.79
Rent of Lands and boxes and hire of Negroes (including Interest) from 15th March A.D. 1850 to 1st January 1854	$1422.32
Sale of Negroes Caesar, Rhoda and Louisa by order of Court April 20th 1852 Interest included	$799.81
Amount of Assets against Exts	$3512.92

Contra

Amount of Vouchers rendered by the Exts including Int to 1st January 1854	$2882.93
Commissions on 3512.92 at 2½ per cent	87.82
Commissions on 2882.93 at 2½ per cent	72.07
Sum Total of Vouchers and Commissions	$3042.82
Amount to be accounted for by Exts	$470.10

The committee show in the foregoing statement that after giving credit for the amount of Vouchers and Allowing Commissions on the Assets and disbursments The Exts are accountable for the sum of four hundred and seventy dollars and ten cents $470.10 January 1st 1854

Bryan W. Hening
R. Pearsall } Committee

In the name of God Amen. Know all men by these presents that I William Stokes of the County of Duplin and State of North Carolina being in a low state of health, but of perfect mind and memory, calling to mind the mortality of my body and knowing it is appointed unto man once to die. Commend my soul unto the hands of Almighty God who Give it and my body to be burried in decent christian burial at the discretion of my executors as takeing such worldly Goods as God has blesed me with do now bequeath and despose of them as follows.

Article 1st, after all my debts are paid I leave unto my well beloved wife Helen Stokes during her natural life and then to despose of as she sees proper, my plantation farming utensels, Houschold & Kitching Furniture and stock property of every Kind except so much of my perishable property as will be necessary to pay my debts.

2nd I leave and bequeath unto my well beloved wife Helen Stokes the seven following named negroes, viz Lot, Mike, Shade, little Lot Sarah, Mima & Kitty, & when she departs this life the land is to be equally devided my between my two youngest children James G Stokes & Priscilla Ann Stokes & also the negroes she cans dispose of them as she sees proper

3rd I leave and bequeath unto my Grand son William Kinsey Stokes one negro girl named Jenice

4 I leave and bequeath unto my well beloved son Joseph Stokes twenty Dollars to be raised out of my estate.

5 I leave and bequeath unto my well beloved daughter Nancy Wells one negro women named Cloe and all her Children by Ervin Violet Isaac Henry Saiah salter Roger Rose Tim & Jerry all of

				336.86
	16.15	Brot Forward		~~346.86~~
	10	10 Bushels Potatoes	Sylvanus Jones	3.00
	30	20 " Potatoes	La Fayette Hapy	5.45
	10	2 Banks Slips	Edward Smith	10.45
	5	1 Ditto	Widow	5
	10	10 Bushels Potatoes	Edward Smith	2.60
	10	10 " "	Wm B Sutherland	2.20
	15	Hire of Nathan until till January Court Week next	John Rhodes	7.25
	10	Claiborne	Edward Smith	11.25
	9.25	Aaron	Widow	5
	2.00	54 Bbls Turpentine	Edward Smith	108.00
	~~24.00~~	Scrape on the Trees	John Smith	51.00
	25	2 Bee Hives	Bryan Kennedy	2.30
	2.25	1 Lot Lumber	J H Mercer	14.86
	50			~~579.32~~
	10	A/c of the Negroes Sold 19th Jany 1858	#	555.32
	2.05	~~Claiborne~~	John Smith	2.55
	2.00	Nathan	Brian Smith	2.01
	80	Aaron	John R Miller	3.51
	5	Joe hired to untill 20 Jany 1858	Elizabeth Miller	2.05
	50			$1491.32
	5		Isaac B Kelly Admr	1467.32
	~~36.95~~			
	$~~36.95~~			

— which are now in her possession

6" I leave and bequeath unto my well beloved daughter Mary James one bed and furniture, she having received her distribution share of my estate by deed of gift already

7 I leave and bequeath unto my well beloved daughter Elizabeth Wells the following named negroes, viz Charity and her two children and a boy named Lewis all of which are in her possession,

8 I leave and bequeath unto my well beloved son James G Stoakes two negroes one named Jim, being a fellow the other a girl named Margaret

9 I leave and bequeath unto my well beloved daughter Priscilla Ann Stoakes one bed and furniture she having allready received her distributive share of my estate by deed of gift,   (James G Stoakes)

10th I constitute and appoint my beloved son James Boney Wells my Executors to this my last will and testament, in manner and form following in witness whereinto I have set my hand this 30 of August 1833   William Stoakes (Seal)

Test Andrew Stoakes

In the name of God. Amen.

I Archilues Branch of the County of Duplin in the State of North Carolina being infirm of body, but of sound and disposing mind and memory, do make and publish this my last Will and testament in manner and form following Towit. First, I commend my Soul to God who gave it, trusting in the merits of Christ for its future welfare, and my body to a burial at the discretion of my surviving friends — As to the worldly estate which I have been favored with, I dispose of as follows, viz —

First, I wish my Executors to sell my Land on Tuffords branch known as the Sullivan Lands, my negro woman Ceily and her child Sarah, my Stock of all kinds, household & kitchen furniture, plantation tools &c at six months credit, and the proceeds of said Sale, together with what money & notes & accounts I may have on hand at my death to be applied to the payment of my debts funeral charges &c —

Item, I give & bequeath to my daughter Clary A. Daniel five dollars in Cash to be raised out of my estate, which together with what I have heretofore given her is to be considered her full share of my estate —

Item, I give & bequeath to my ~~daughter Clary Daniel~~ son James G. Branch my negro man Isom, and one half of all my Lands not mentioned before to be to him and his heirs forever —

Item, I give & bequeath to my son James G. Branch & my friend Daniel Herring in trust for the benefit of my son Archilaus Bright Branch the one half of my Lands

2.

property heretofore bequeathed a devised to the said

I now devise that the said James Dickson be disposed of as follows, to-wit: The 400 acres of land since the desease of the said James I have sold for the sum of $400. which as soon as due and collected, to be laid out on interest for the use of the said James's three dauthters, Maria, Eliza, and Patsey. And the said negro man Spencer, to be sold by my Executors at their discretion after my desease as soon as may be convenient, and *Money* arising from the sale of the said Spencer, to be laid out on interest for the use of the said Maria, Eliza, and Patsey, and may at any time at the discretion of my Executors herein after named, with the consent of Elenor Dickson, the mother of the said Maria, Eliza, and Patsey, be appointed to the purchase of young slaves for the use of the said Maria, Eliza and Patsey and the said slaves or monies to be equally devided between them as they attain to the age of twenty one years or marry which may *first* happen, to them, their heirs and assigns forever:— And as by a former will I had devised and bequeathed to my son Lewis Dickson, my Manor Plantation whereon I now live, lying on the South side and in Goshen Swamp including all my lands adjoining thereto, with all my buildings, orchards, &c. thereon, lying between and bounded by the lands of David Wright, Joseph Dickson, Elisha Herring, Elias Faison, Lewis Dickson and David Hooks, containing in the whole by estimation seven hundred and thirty acres be it more or less. And also my Negro Slaves, to-wit, Cato, old Ned and old Caesar; and my said son Lewis Dickson being since deceased, and having left legal issue, two Infant Daughters, to-wit; Patsey and Eliza; I now will and bequeath to the said Patsey and Eliza, my said Manor plantation, and all my lands, thereto adjoining and belonging as herein bounded and described and containing in the whole by estimation seven hundred and thirty acres be it more or less, to be equally divided between them the said Patsey Dickson and Eliza Dickson

Dickson, William 1820

Caroline's future increase.

Item 2nd I give and bequeath to my brother Wright Boney my negro boy Enoch girl Francinia my woman Julia and her two youngest children Margaret & Ellen and all Julia's future increase.

3rd I give and bequeath to my sister Susan Sloan my negro girls Indie & Emily.

4th I give and bequeath to my sister Mary Boney, my negro girls Linda & Chloe.

5th I give and bequeath to my sister Catharine A. Stoake, my negro girl Patsey also my woman Aly and her two children Tom and Jane, and all Aly's future increase.

Lastly I do hereby constitute and appoint my brother Wells Boney and my brother-in-law James S. Soake, my lawful executors to all intents and purposes to execute this my last Will and testament according to the true intent and meaning of the same and every part and clause thereof — hereby revoking and declaring utterly void all other Wills and testaments by me heretofore made. In Witness Whereof I the said William Boney do hereunto set my hand and seal this 28th day of Nov. A.D. 1853.

William Boney (Seal)

Signed Sealed published and declared by the said William Boney to be his last Will and testament in the presence of us who at his request and in his presence do subscribe our names as Witnesses thereto

Hanson F. Murphey
John W. Carr

I William Boney of the County of Duplin and State of North Carolina being of sound mind and memory but considering the uncertainty of my earthly existence do make and publish this my last Will and testament in manner and form following that is to say:

First — That my executors (herein after named) shall provide for my body a decent burial suitable to the wishes of my relations and friends and pay all funeral expenses, together with my just debts howsoever and to whomsoever owing out of the moneys that may first come into their hands as a part or parcel of my estate.

Item 1st I give and bequeath to my brother Wells Boney the plantation on which I reside including my dwelling house all out houses, grist mill and all the improvements and appurtenances to sd plantation together with all my household and kitchen furniture—. Also all my right title interest and privileges on a tract of Turpentine land bequeathed by the Will of my father Jno Boney to my Mother Mary Boney brother Wells and myself in common. I give and bequeath to my brother Wells Boney my negroes namies as follows Jacob, Pat, Caroline and her three children Anne, Dempsey and Sarah Eliza and all arisen amongst my Heirs Concerning the said Negro Slave Sidney and her Son Jackson, I hereby Will, and ordain as follows.

I Give and bequeath to my Grand Daughter Maria Lanier the Daughter of William and Ann Lanier, my Negro Woman Slave Sidney, with all the future increase from this date, to her the said Maria Lanier, her Heirs and Assigns for ever.

I Give and bequeath to my Grand Daughter Susanna Lanier, the Daughter of William and Ann Lanier, my Negro boy Slave called Jackson, to her the said Susanna Lanier, her Heirs and Assigns for ever. —

And I hereby declare this Codicil to be a part of my foregoing Last Will and Testament, and to have the same force and Effect as the other Clauses therein.

Signed, Sealed, pronounced and declared by the said William Dickson the Testator to be a part of the foregoing Will. — In presence of us.

D. Wright
Ann Dickson
Ann Pearsall

Wm Dickson (Seal)

William Dickson's
Will
20th Sept 1816

Recorded
July Term 1820

Book A Page 109.

State of N. Carolina } In the name of God, Amen!
Duplin County   I John Boney of the state and
county aforesaid, Being sick and infirm in body;
But Blessed be God, of perfect mind & memory;
Calling to mind the uncertainty of Life, and the
certainty of Death; For the better regulation of
my earthly business, Do make & ordain this my
last will & testament, in form as follows:—
In the first place, I commend my soul to God who
gave it; And my body to its Mother earth.—
Of the earthly goods I enjoy, I will & ordain to
be distributed in the following manner, namely:
1st I give and bequeath unto my loving Wife Mary
Boney, during her natural life, all my Lands,
east of my mills, including the grist Mill; And at
her demise, to my son William Boney— I likewise
give & bequeath unto my said Wife Mary: The following negroes, viz Bill, Sarah, Phebe & Maria,
with the following stock, Six cows, my stock of Hogs,
Sheep, two Horses, Plantation & Farming tools,
Household & Kitchen furniture &c &c to have, as her
own during her natural life, as above; And at
her demise, all the aforesaid perishable property,
(excepting Maria) I will & ordain, to my two

In the name of God amen. I William Boney Sent., of the State of North Carolina & County of Duplin, being weak in body, but, thanks to almighty God, of sound mind and memory, at this time & calling to mind that all men are mortal & must die I by this my last will and testament first of all recommend my soul to God who gave it, and my body to be buried in a christian like manner at the discretion of my Executors hereinafter named; and the worldly goods with which it hath pleased God to bless me I shall dispose of in the manner & form following. Viz. First of all my just debts to be paid out of my Estate by my Executors. &

2nd I give & bequeath unto my beloved wife Dorothy Boney all the remaining part of my lands adjoining the place whereon I now live not especially conveyd by deed &c, during her natural life & afterwards to be divided equally among all my children. Also so much of the plantation tools & house hold & kitchen furniture as she may really need, & one Horse & Chair, One Yoke of Oxen & Cart. Four Cows & Calves, Four Sows & twenty Pigs or Shoats, & of the Corn & Meat on hand, so much as will last until gathering time & the remainder to be divided equally amongst all my children. after enough of my Corn & Meat & Stock has been sold to defray expenses. As to my Negro's not already conveyed I give unto my wife Dorothy Four negroes namely Dilly, Flora, Jenny & Jurrismow to take care of the old negro Dinah. These negroes I give during her

turn over

In the name of God amen

I Elizabeth Dobson of the County of Duplin and State of Northcarolina Being aged and infurm But Sound in mind and memory and Caling to mind that it is ordaind for all people onest to Die, thearfore I make this my last will and testament in maner and form as folow to wit

Item I Give and Bequeth my Soul to almighty god who give it and my Body to the Dust from whence it Com to Be Buried in a Christan like manner at the Discretion of my Surviving friend

Item After paying my Just Debts and funeral Expen=ses I give to my Daughter Sally Grimeses Children one Dolor

Item I Give to my Daughter Alsa Dumpseys Children one Dolor

Item I give to my Daughter Nancy Joneses Children one Dolor

Item My will is that my Negro woman Lidda my Stock of all kind my household and Kitchen furniture Be Equely Devided Between my three Sones John Dobson James Dobson and Peory Dobson — My will is that my three Sones above named Settle and Devides my Estate as they think proper

Signed and Sealed in presants of David Southerland

Elizabeth (her mark) Dobson

Lavinia Killpatrick

this the 11th of June 1845

I Richard Miller of the County of Duplin and
State of North Carolina being of sound mind
and memory but considering the uncertainty of
my earthly existance do make and declare this my
last Will and testament in manner and form following that is to say

First — I lend a 4 horse farm to my beloved Wife
during her natural life time and the following
Negroes Frank & his wife Hanna and her two Boys
Harvy & Rodger Mary and her daughter Harriet and
her Son Sip, big Clary and her three daughters Luce
Jane & Linda, Daniel & Malvina the ballance to be
hired out in common stock until the Heirs arrive at
the age of twenty one or marry. Ben & his wife Miles
Old Sarah & John I wish kept & supported on the farm
The above mentioned farm I wish to be selected by
my Executors or two more persons of good Judgment
5,000 lbs of Bacon One barrel lard 3 Barrels flour one
Barrel fish One barrel Sugar One bag Coffee One barrel
molasses 150 Barrels Corn 10 bushels Salt 30 bushels
peas all my Slips 20 Head Cattle 5 Sows & pigs 20
head Shoats all the Sheep & Horses her Choice all
the poultry of every kind all my House and Kitchen
furniture My Barouch & harness One Waggon
and all plows and axes 6 grubbing hoes 2 Spades 2 Shovels
2 forks and all the weeding hoes grind Stone and
all the Blacksmith tools.

Item — I give and devise unto my three Sons Richard
Eleas, Stephen Henry, & John William all the lands I
posess except my Interest in my Brother George's land
in Florida that I wish Sold by my Executors and
the money applied to the benefit of all my children
and my Will is that they shall pay over to the two
Girls Martha Francis and Mary Winefred

all and Singular a Tract or Parcel of land Patented by myself, and Sold apart to Benjamin Johnston and James Toney, and the Ballance I give to Thomas Kenan, him and his Heirs forever. —

Item. I give and bequeath to my Daughter Sarah Kenan my Negro Wench Thena and all her Children to her and her Heirs forever.

Item. I give and bequeath to my Daughter Jane Kenan my Negro Wench Hagar and her Children and also my Negro boy Isaac to her and her Heirs forever.

Item. I give and bequeath to my Grand Daughter Sarah Norment, my Negro boy Ireland.

Item. It is also my Will and desire, that my Executors, dispose of and Sell as they may think proper such part of my Stock to discharge my debts; And all the Rest of my Estate consisting of Negroes, Cattle, Hogs, Sheep, Horses, Plantation Tools, Kitchen furniture of every kind, and all my Household furniture, I leave to my wife Sarah during her Natural Life; And at her Death, to be Equally divided amongst all my Children, (that is to say) the Shares drawn by Elizabeth Price, my Daughter and Susanna Green my Daughter, I Will and bequeath to their Children, to be Equally divided amongst them and to no others.

And it is my Will, If Catharine Kenan should Survive my wife Sarah She shall be maintained out of my Estate.

I do hereby Constitute and appoint Thomas

I Richard Miller of the County of Duplin and
State of North Carolina being of sound mind
and memory but considering the uncertainty of
my earthly existance do make and declare this my
last Will and testament in manner and form following that is to say

First — I lend a 4 horse farm to my beloved Wife
during her natural life time and the following
Negroes Frank & his wife Henna and her two Boys
_____ & _____ Mary and her daughter Harriet and
her son Sip, Big Clary and her three daughters Luce
Jane & Linda, Daniel & Malvina The ballance to be
hired out in common Stock until the Heirs arrive at
the age of twenty one or marry. Ben & his wife Mila
Old Sarah & John I wish kept & supported on the farm
The above mentioned farm I wish to be selected by
my Executors or two more persons of good Judgment
5.000 lbs of Bacon One barrel lard 3 Barrels flour one
Barrel fish One barrel Sugar One bag Coffee One barrel
Molases 150 Barrels Corn 10 bushels Salt 30 bushels
peas all my Slips 20 Head Cattle 5 Sows & pigs 20
head Shots all the Sheep 4 Horses her choice all
the poultry of every kind all my House and Kitchen
furniture my Barouch & harness One Waggon
_____ all _____ axes 6 grubbing hoes 2 Spades 2 Shovels
2 forks and all the weeding hoes grind stone and
all the Blacksmith tools

Item — I give and devise unto my three Sons Richard
Eleas, Stephen Henry, & John William all the lands I
posses except my Interest in my Brother George's land
in Florida, that I wish sold by my Executors and
the money applied to the benefit of all my children
and my Will is that they shall pay over to the two
Girls Martha Francis and Mary Winefred

AFRICAN AMERICAN Heritage

DUPLIN COUNTY, NORTH CAROLINA

38

EDUCATION

Mrs. Juanita Butler Boney Class

Rosenwald Fund

Today the structures stand almost forgotten, scattered across the North Carolina countryside. Some are now houses, businesses, or barns. Others—particularly those that stand next to churches as community halls—still retain the large banks of windows that mark them as school buildings. These are Rosenwald Fund schools, landmarks in the history of Afro-American education.

Conceived in the 1910s by black educator Booker T. Washington and his Tuskegee Institute staff, the Rosenwald program represented a massive effort to improve black rural schooling in the South through public-private partnership. The name came from philanthropist Julius Rosenwald, president of Sears, Roebuck and Company. Rosenwald offered matching grants to rural communities interested in building black schools.

In the short run, the Rosenwald Fund had an impressive effect. By the early 1930s thousands of old shanty schoolhouses had been replaced with new, larger structures constructed from modern standardized plans. Over 5,300 Rosenwald buildings blanketed fifteen southern states. More were erected in North Carolina than in any other state. Through a combination of active leadership in the state Department of Public Instruction and enthusiastic fund raising by blacks at the grass-roots level, North Carolina constructed more over 800 Rosenwald buildings.

Julius Rosenwald

Julius Rosenwald was born August 12, 1862, in Springfield, Illinois, the son of a German-Jewish immigrant who had risen from peddler to partner in a clothing concern. In 1909 Julius Rosenwald became president of Sears, Roebuck and Company, a firm that he joined in 1897. With the personal fortune that he amassed, he also became known as one of America's leading philanthropists.

While Rosenwald supported a wide range of causes, his chief concern became Negro education in the South. . . . Reading a number of books—especially Booker T. Washington's Up from Slavery—had also sparked big interest in charitable works for blacks. After providing matching grants for a handful of black YMCAs, Rosenwald met Washington in 1911 and soon became a trustee of Tuskegee Institute. Initially, Booker T. Washington's Tuskegee Institute staff administered the Rosenwald program. . . . By

1920, however, the burgeoning construction program was more than Tuskegee could handle, and Julius Rosenwald created the Rosenwald "Southern Office" in Nashville, Tennessee. To run it he hired Samuel Leonard Smith, who not only had a decade's experience administering Tennessee's rural Negro school program but also possessed a keen interest in country schoolhouse design.

Washington persuaded Rosenwald that help was needed not just with higher education as offered at Tuskegee but with elementary schools throughout the South. When on the occasion of Rosenwald's fiftieth birthday the tycoon presented Washington with $25,000 to aid black colleges and preparatory academies, the black educator asked to use a small amount for grants to black communities near Tuskegee that wanted to build rural elementary schools. Rosenwald agreed, stipulating that each community had to raise its own funds to match the gift. In 1913 the first "Rosenwald School" was dedicated in Alabama. By the time that Booker T. Washington died in 1915,

Rosenwald had already personally given matching money for some eighty black schools in a three-state area. Two years later Rosenwald established the Julius Rosenwald Fund to continue and expand his charitable activities. . . .

Bealuhvile School

Bealuhville School read view

Bealuhville School Payground

Duplin County

Rosenwald Schools

42

Big Zion School

Big Zion School Bakside

Chinquapin High School

Duplin County Rosenwald Schools

Chinquapin Elementary School

Branch School

Wallace School

Duplin County Rosenwald Schools

Grady School

Cobb School

Faison School

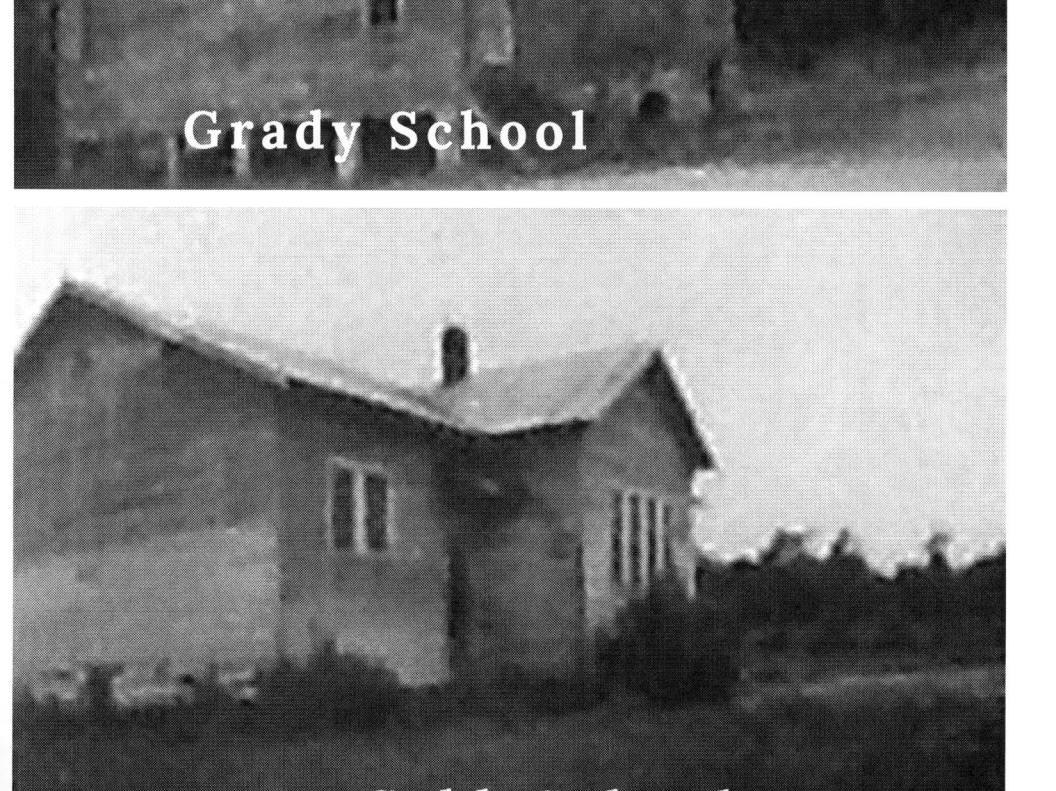

Duplin County Rosenwald Schools

45

Chinquapin School

Warsaw Elementary School

Kenansville School

Duplin County Rosenwald Schools

46

Standford School

Rose Hill School

Island Creek School

Duplin County Rosenwald Schools

47

Calpsyo School

Warsaw High School

Farrior School

Duplin County Rosenwald Schools

Rev. Dr. Ezekial Ezra Smith

E. E. Smith School
Kenansville, North Carolina

E. E. Smith High School was named after Rev. Dr. Ezekial Ezra Smith. He was born May 23, 1852 in Duplin County, North Carolina and he died December 6, 1933 in Fayetteville, Cumberland County, North Carolina. He was the son of Alexander and Caroline Smith. He received a Bachelor's degree from Shaw University in 1878. He served for six years as the Pastor of First Baptist Church in Fayetteville, North Carolina. He served as the president of Fayetteville State Normal School now Fayetteville State University. In 1881 he organized and operated the Carolina Enterprise, the first newspaper in the state for blacks. Later he was editor of the Banner Enterprise and the Baptist Sentinel.

Duplin County
African American School

**Little Creek School
Greenevers, North Carolina.**

North Carolina Digital Collections 1937 - 1946 Duplin County Principals Report for Colored Schools

52

HIGH SCHOOL PRINCIPAL'S ANNUAL REPORT
STATE DEPARTMENT OF PUBLIC INSTRUCTION

YEAR 19 37 - 19 38   RACE Negro

COUNTY Duplin
SCHOOL Rose Hill Jr. High
POST OFFICE Rose Hill, N.C.

Principal: Windsor H. Johnson   Chairman: T. M. Barden
Secretary: C. Russell   State School opened this year August 26, 1937   Closed April 14, 1938

I. LENGTH TERM AND NUMBER TEACHERS

ITEMS	HIGH SCHOOL	ELEMENTARY
Length of term	160	32 Weeks / 160 Days
No. years work given	2	
No. teachers	1	Men — Women 1 Total 1	Men 1 Women 3 Total 4

II. ENROLLMENT BY GRADE, ATTENDANCE, ETC. FOR YEAR

CAUTION: Schools organized on the 7-4 plan will give figures for grades 8-11 only.

Grade	Boys	Girls	Total	Boys	Girls	Total	Boys	Girls	Total
Seventh Grade									
Eighth Grade	10	21	31	6	16	22	6	16	22
Ninth Grade	9	19	28	6	13	19	6	13	19
Tenth Grade									
Eleventh Grade									
Twelfth Grade									
Totals	19	40	59	12	29	41	12	29	41

III. GENERAL INFORMATION

Is building separate from elementary? No
No. classrooms? 6   No. used for H.S. 1
Is there an auditorium? Yes   Principal's office? No
Is there a lunch room? No

Teacher's rest room? No   First aid room? No
Do you have well-kept grounds? No
Will offer graduation? No

IV. LIBRARY

Is there a separate room? No   Size of room 30 x 34
Are books classified? No
Recommended list:
Literature
Total 125
No. Magazines 3   Daily papers 1

Wallace Colored High School,
Wallace, North Carolina.
November 18, 1937.

Mr. H.L. Trigg
State Department of Education,
Raleigh, North Carolina.

Dear Mr. Trigg:

We were very glad to have you visit our school a few days ago, but I very much regret the fact that I was away at the time. I am glad however, that as a results of my being away we were able to complete plans and order a school bus for our district October the 28th. We hope that this bus will soon be on hand.

We shall be glad to supply you with any other information you may desire.

I am very truly yours,

C.W. Dobbins.

DATE: Nov. 19, 1937

1. Name and Location: Wallace Col. School, Wallace, N.C.

2. School Pop: County _____

   Area to be served   35 sq. mi.

   Adequate for Accreditment _____

   Location in county   Southern end of county

3. Enrollment: High   74   Elementary: 253

4. Term High: 36 wks.   Elementary: 36 wks.

5. Length of Recitation periods: 50

6. Teachers High: 3   Elementary: 6

   C.W. Dobbins   ; Irene A. Williams
   J.H. Draughon   ; Jettie V. Summersett
   Visel Savage   ; Mary F. Lewis
                               ; Catharyne Closson
                               ; Mattie M. Pierce
                               ; Isabella McGowen

7. Building: No. Rooms High   3   Elementary: 6   Condition: Fair

8. Library Room: 1, 21 X 30 ft. Equipment: 3 tables&ch., 330 shelves

9. Textbooks: _____

10. Major Phys. _____ FCL: _____ B.B.O: _____

11. Office Room: _____ Filing Case: _____ Record: _____

12. Are teachers teaching subjects for which they are certificated?   Yes

13. Interested Negro citizens: Mr. J.W. Powers
                                 Mr. Clifton Hammonds
                                 Mrs. Lillie Pearsall
                                 Mr. Arthor Hayes
                                 Mr. B. Underwood

DATE: Nov. 19, 1957

1. Name and Location: Wallace Col. School, Wallace, N.C.
2. School Jep: County
   Area to be served: 35 sq. mi.
   Adequate for Accreditment:
   Location in county: Southern end of county
3. Enrolment: High 78   Elementary: 235
4. Term High: 36 wks.   Elementary: 36 wks.
5. Length of Recitation periods: 60
6. Teachers High: 3   Elementary: 6

   C.W. Dobbins   ; Irene A. Williams
   J.H. Draughon   ; Jettie V. Summersett
   Visel Savage   ; Mary F. Lewis
                         ; Catharyne Closson
                         ; Mattie M. Pierce
                         ; Isabella McGowen

7. Building: No. Rooms High 3   Elementary: 6   Condition: Fair
8. Library Room: 1, 21 X 30 ft Equipment: 3 tables, 350 shelves
9. Textbooks:
10. Maps: Phys.   Pol: B.S.C:
11. Office Room: Filing Case: Record:
12. Are teachers teaching subjects for which they are certificated? Yes
13. Interested Negro citizens: Mr. J.M. Powers
                               Mr. Clifton Hammonds
                               Mrs. Lillie Pearsall
                               Mr. Arthor Hayes
                               Mr. R. Underwood

HIGH SCHOOL PRINCIPAL'S ANNUAL REPORT
STATE DEPARTMENT OF PUBLIC INSTRUCTION
YEAR 1937-1938   RACE Negro

COUNTY Pender
SCHOOL Topsail School
POST OFFICE Penson, N.C.

Principal J. N. Harden   School opened this year Aug. 26, 1937   Closed April 19, 1938

I. LENGTH TERM AND NUMBER TEACHERS

ITEMS	HIGH SCHOOL	ELEMENTARY
Length of term	8 mos / 36 weeks / 160 days	
No. teachers	3 — Men 1, Women 2, Total 3	Women 4, Total 4

II. ENROLLMENT BY GRADE, ATTENDANCE, ETC. FOR YEAR

Grade	Enrolled Boys	Girls	Total	Attendance Boys	Girls	Total	Promoted Boys	Girls	Total
Eighth	12	24	36	10	19	29	8	18	26
Ninth	8	21	29	6	17	23	17	22	39
Tenth	3	11	14	2	7	9	1	7	8
Eleventh		7	7		4	4		7	6
Totals	23	63	86	18	47	65	16	51	67

Number of Graduates: Boys 0, Girls 4, Total 4

III. GENERAL INFORMATION
- Is building separate from elementary? Yes
- No. classrooms: 6   No. used for H.S.: 3
- Is there an auditorium? Yes   Principal's office? Yes
- Is there a lunch room? No
- Teacher's rest room? No   First aid room? No
- Mid-year graduation? No

IV. LIBRARY
- Is there a separate room? Yes   Size: 12 x 18
- Are books classified? Yes

STATE DEPARTMENT OF PUBLIC INSTRUCTION
RALEIGH, NORTH CAROLINA

__Wallace Colored__ High School Library

__Duplin__ County

__April 12, 1938__ Date

SUBJECT	CLASSIFICATION	REQUIRED	ON HAND	NEED
Approved Encyclopedia	030	20 (1 set)	10	
Gov, Civics, Economics	300	10	15	
Language Unabridged English Dictionary	420	1	1	
Foreign Language Dictionary		1 ea.lang. taught	1 (French)	
Science	500	25	29	
Useful Arts (If Home Ec. and Agri. are taught)	600	10	10	
Fine Arts	700	10	10	
Literature	100,200,800	25	25	
Poetry	821	20	20	
Geography and Travel	900-919	25	27	
History and Biography	920-999	75	73	2
Fiction	F,398,SC	75	73	2
Atlas	912	1	2	
Standard Catalog for High School Libraries (Abridged edition)	010	1	—	
Miscellaneous			30	
		TOTAL	326	

VIII. LABORATORIES

	Total Value	Value of Apparatus Only
General Science	$130	$100
Biology	$190	$150
Geography		
Chemistry		
Physics	$350	$300
Agriculture		
Home Economics		
Commercial		
Manual Training		
Any other		
Totals		

Is desk apparatus used for laboratory? **No**

Size of room?

IX. MAPS AND GLOBE

A. Physical (political) Author
   Publisher **Rand McNally & Co.** No. **6**

B. Political Author
   Publisher   No.

C. Physical Author
   Publisher   No.

D. Blackboard Outline Publisher   No.

E. Historical Author
   Publisher **Rand McNally & Co.** No. **4**

F. History Charts Maker
                                              No.

G. Map of North Carolina Publisher   No. **1**

H. Globes No.   Size   Publisher
   Type of stand in mounting

X. EXTRA-CURRICULAR

Is there a teacher of Physical Education? **No** Gymnasium? **No**
Is Physical Education required of all pupils? **No**
Is a coach employed? **Yes** Whole time? **No** Part time? **Yes**
Are pupils taking part in:
Football?   Baseball? **30** Tennis?   Basketball? **44** Track?
Other sports?
Name prize debaters?
Name boys orators?
Name school magazine?
Name school newspaper?
Give number pupils in clubs:
Boys Glee Club? **8**   Girls Glee Club? **24**
Literary Society: Boys   Girls
Hi-Y?   Dramatic Club?
Other clubs: **Crown & Scepter Club and Science Club**

XII. REMARKS:

XI. GRADUATES (Senior High School only)

Give names of graduates, arranged alphabetically. Not necessary to give address. Use separate sheet if necessary.

Boys	Girls
Dixon, James Willie	Baney, Maggie
Moore, James	Branch, Minnie
Smith, Edward James	Carlton, Elma
	Carlton, Rosa
	Carlton, Eula
	Cooper, Mary Lou
	Frederick, Emma
	McColope, Clennie
	McColope, Norma
	Martin, Pearl
	Rich, Callie Bell
	Smith, Nattie Lillian
	Smith, Josephine
	Smith, Maree
	Smith, Nora
	Wilson, Crettie
	Wilson, Vera
	Williams, Zula

For last year's graduates give the following:
Total number **13**
No. entering college or university **4**
No. entering normal or technical school **1**
No. entering Business College

I hereby certify the foregoing report is correct to the best of my knowledge and belief.

Date   (Signed) **M. S. Branch** Principal
                                           (Approved) **C. J. Johnson** Superintendent

60

FAMILY HISTORIES

John Heaton Carr was born in 1865 and he died in 1915 in Rose Hill, Duplin County, North Carolina. He is the son of Richard Carr and Annie Lucinda Jane Carr. He married Sophronia Boney. She was born in 1866 and she died in 1955. She is the daughter of Henry Carr and Betsy Boney. From this union eight children were born.

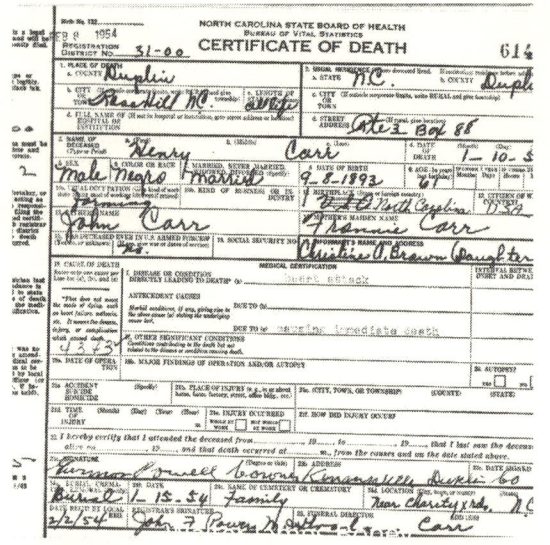

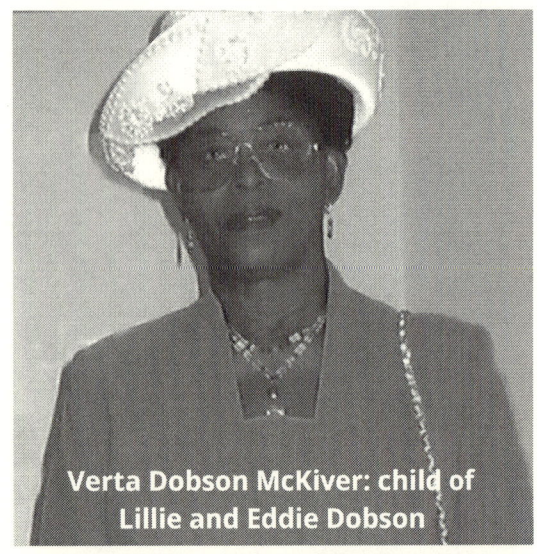

Henry Richard Carr & Eliza Sykes
February 8, 1891 - January 10, 1954

Lillie J. Carr & Eddie Dobson
May 11, 1895 - November 20, 1990

Cummie Hayes Carr & Herman Daniel Chasten
August 9, 1897 - April 15, 1972

James Rhodes Carr & Beatrice Murray
May 16, 1902 - December 8, 1981

Betsy Pearl Carr & Willie Batts
April 10, 1902 - June 15, 1996

Nancy Mae Carr & Clifton Boney
September 27, 1903 - March 25, 1971

John Heaton Carr Jr. & Vivian E. Bryant
October 5, 1905 - July 2, 1972

Jessie David Carr & Mary Caroline Mae Batts
1909 - July 27, 1968

Verta Dobson McKiver: child of Lillie and Eddie Dobson

Doctor Twille Dobson: child of Lillie and Eddie Dobson

John Thomas Boney was born in May of 1854 and he died November 30, 1922 in Teachy, Duplin County, North Carolina. He is the son of Robert & Grace Boney. He married Julia Ann Pearsall. She was born in February of 1858 and she died July 20, 1940 in Teachy, Duplin County, North Carolina. She is the daughter of Horace and Polly Pearsall. From this union six children were born.

James Boney Sr. & Susan Ann McGee
April 5, 1881 - 1972

Robert Horace Boney & Mary Elizabeth Sheffield
December 12, 1882 - November 10, 1962

Polly Jane Boney & Sanders Sheffield
July 29, 1887 - January 20, 1943

Earl Boney & Cora Robinson
February 1888 - May 26, 1961

Walter James Boney Sr. & Illa Frances Costen
December 3, 1892 - September 18, 1955

Abbie Boney Herring & Garlie Chasten
June 15, 1894 - October 24, 1944

Walter James Boney

Robert Horace Boney

Annie Boney Chasten Herring

John Boda James Jr. was born February of 1854 and he died July 4, 1932 in Rosehill, Duplin County, North Carolina. He is the son of John and Hannah James. He married Margaret Murray August 22, 1875 in Duplin County, North Carolina. She was born in May of 1853 and she died around 1907. From this union eight children were born.

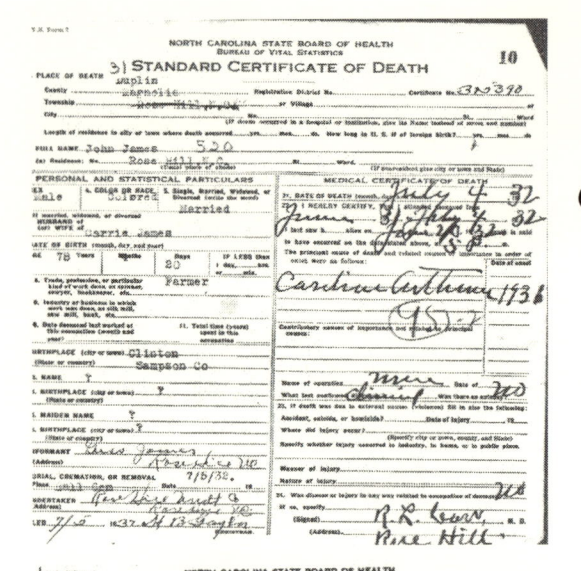

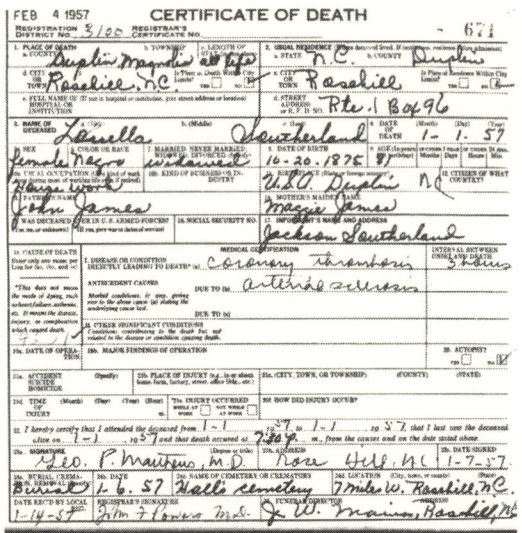

Luella James & Frank Southerland
October 20, 1875 - January 1, 1957

Carrie Lena Idella James & Joseph Thomas Bright
November 1877 - August 25, 1933

John B. James & Ann Julia Underwood
November 1879 - August 7, 1930

William Arthur James & Dilcia E. Williams
July 21, 1892 - June 3, 1942

John Boba & Dosia James
May 11, 1885 - August 7, 1930

Augustus James & Anna Stokes
August 5, 1889 - February 1, 1985

Henry James & Eva Merritt
June 21, 1893 - December 7, 1953

Maggie E. James & Lafayette Williams
May 26, 1896 - July 21, 1961

James Martin Robinson was born in March of 1846 and he died in 1916. He married Sarah Chasten. She was born May 2, 1854 and she died August 3, 1917. She is the daughter of Isaac Chasten & Sarah Kilpatrick (Hollingsworth). From this union seven children were born.

Rosanna V. Robinson & Lott M. Murray
November 1873 - July 13, 1931

Rufus James Robinson & Carrie Hill
March 13, 1879 - July 19, 1946

Kezia Robinson
1885

Joicy Ann Robinson & Kellem Hill
January 7, 1888 - February 5, 1921

Arnett B. Robinson & Flora Highsmith
January 8, 1889 - November 8, 1925

Isaac Jacob Robinson & Margie Anna Murphy
June 15, 1892 - January 1966

Fannie Bell Robinson & Sylvester Murray
June 13, 1894 - June 14, 1981

Issac Jacob Robinson

James Martin Robison great grandson of James Martin & Sarah Robinson

James Needham Dobson was born in May of 1848 and he died August 21, 1934 in Duplin County, North Carolina. He is the son of Amos L. Dobson and Susan Ann Grant. He married Clara Middleton February 4, 1880 in Duplin County, North Carolina. She is the daughter of Jerry and Elsie Middleton. From this union thirteen children were born.

Annie Ruth Dobson Southerland

Elijah Tommie Dobson

General Needham Dobson

James David Dobson & Annie Graham
March 23, 1881 - June 23, 1958

John Dobson
March 7, 1882 - March 21, 1958

Susan Ann Dobson & Barney Hall
February 26, 1884 - May 19, 1945

Alex Steven Dobson & Dora Wells
July 8, 1885 - June 3, 1984

William Henry Dobson & Louise McIver
1889

Elijah Thomas Dobson & Narcissus Hall
January 31, 1885 - February 12, 1976

Eddie Dobson & Lillie Carr & Bell McAuthur
April 9, 1891 - February 18, 1969

Cissero Dobson & Corlattie Mathis, Mary Emma Faison
January 8, 1892 - August 16, 1984

Octave Dobson & Elizabeth Smith Williams
May 5, 1894 - March 2, 1972

General Needham Dobson & Mary Catherine McAuthur
December 15, 1895 - March 24, 1983

Carrie Dobson & Joe Smith
February 1900 - May 23, 1962

Daniel L. Dobson & Mattie Monk Williams
October 10, 1900 - February 18, 1967

Rosa Lee Dobson & Stanford Kea
July 2, 1910 - May 28, 1923

Haywood Newkirk was born in 1853 and he died in 1913. He is the son of Essex and Pearcy Matthews. He married Phoebe J. Kenan on September 11, 1886 in Duplin County, North Carolina. She was born in 1852 and she died in 1923. She is the daughter of Mary Kenan. From this union 10 children were born.

Nancy Ann Kenan & Isaac Furlow
1876 -

Ida Kenan McMillan
1878 - 1959

James Owen Newkirk & Bettie Wells
July 10, 1878 - October 24, 1983

Lula Clyde Newkirk & Ree Trevan Hall
April 1883 - November 28, 1921

Sarah Newkirk & Conovia Farrior
June 21, 1885 - September 10, 1951

Annie Belle Newkirk & Roscoe Pickett
1888 - July 2, 1957

Rosco Newkirk & Amanda Newkirk
September 12, 1890 - August 26, 1978

Cora Newkirk & Hessie Waters
February 11, 1899 - January 11, 1987

William C. Newkirk & Bessie Peyton
March 7, 1897 - July 24, 1954

Catherine Ann Murray was born in January of 1862 and she died April 4, 1943. She is the daughter of Jack Murray and Louvenia Wallace. She married Hicks Stalling. He was born in 1852 and he died September 1, 1935. From this union eleven children were born.

Lucinda Stallings & William Henry Kidd
February 1881 - December 29, 1965

Louvinia Stallings & Gibson Pigford
1894

Kittie Ann Stallings McMillan
1895 - 1959

John Soloman Stallings
April 3, 1900 - December 1, 1944

Ida Stallings
October 12, 1903 - January 13, 1961

Winnie Stallings & Ernest McGee
January 10, 1905 - February 23, 1944

Sarah Stallings and Edward Savage
1898

Soloman Stallings
October 3, 1898 - October 16, 1963

Bright Stallings
1903 - January 14, 1922

James Arthur Stallings
January 10, 1889 - January 13, 1961

Jerry Hicks Stalling & Arinda Stallings
August 29, 1906 - March 1985

Caldonia (Callie) Kenan was born in March of 1896 and she died November 19, 1955. She is the daughter of Lewis Kenan and Lucy Stanford. She married Arnold Murray. He was born in 1860 and no death date was found on him. He is the son of Jack Murray and Levinia Teachy. From this union five children were born:

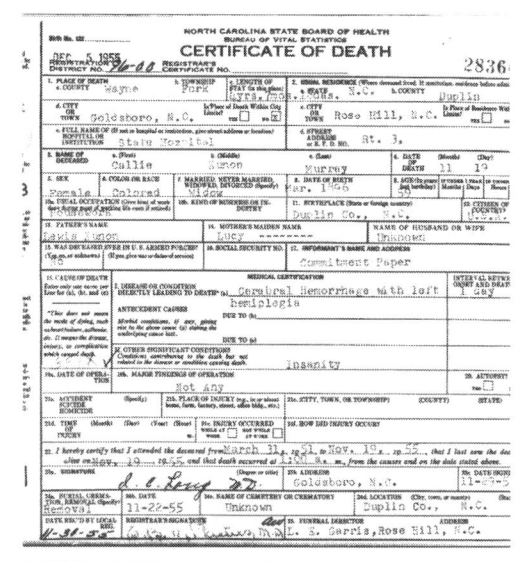

Janie B. Murray & Leroy Spicer
April 15, 1920 - March 29, 2012

Mabel Murray & John Branch
June 17, 1925 - November 26, 2000

Stacy Murray & Pearlie Purcell
July 17, 1927 - April 15, 1994

Sudie Murray & Jessie Wooten
1930 - January 17, 2013

Arnold Murray
1937

Albert Pickett was born February 12, 1859 and he died March 8, 1921 in Chinqupin, Duplin County, North Carolina. He is the son of Anthony Friday Pickett and Merinda Becton. He married Chelsey Kenan. She was born in May of 1866 and she died April 8, 1925. She is the daughter of Charlie Kenan and Charlotte Graham. From this union eight children were born.

Laura Pickett & Soloman Williams
1881

Luther Pickett & Pennie Pickett
December 25, 1883 - April 18, 1949

Caleb Pickett
May 3, 1886 - February 6, 1950

Roscoe Pickett & Annie Bell Newkirk
June 30, 1887 - September 27, 1962

Amelia Pickett & Wesley Moore
November 30, 1889 - October 25, 1980

Nola Pickett & Henry Barden
March 26, 1893 - July 22, 1923

Charlotte Pickett
1897

Naomi (Sing) Pickett & George Washington Graham
1900

70

Abram Harrison Dixon was born September 20, 1869 and he died November 20, 1942. He is the son of Samuel Dixon and Hannah Farrior. He married Lucy Ann Graham. She was born in January of 1874 and she died June 6, 1960. She is the daughter of Thomas and Caroline Graham. From this union eleven children were born.

William Alton Dixon & Mary Corbett
June 25, 1895 - May 28, 1984

Kalie E. Dixon & Garlie Chasten
1901 - August 16, 1925

Hullie C. Dixon & Louvenia Boney
1902 - 1979

Hannah F. Dixon & Alexander Williams
January 3, 1904 - 1980

Thomas Theodore Dixon & Georgia A. McArthur
January 10, 1907 - January 18, 1986

Macy C. Dixon
1908

Ludie Dixon & Vander Washington
July 20, 1909 - January 16, 1988

Harriett A. Dixon
1910

Viola G. Dixon
1910 - August 27, 1937

Arthur Lassie Dixon
October 28, 1914 - 1978

Dorothy P. Dixon
1915

Jim (James) Stephen Stokes was born was born May 17, 1858 and he died August 19, 1942. He is the son of Mike Stokes (Usher) and Margaret Dixon. He married Marinday Moore. She was born February 15, 1872 and she died January 27, 1916. She is the daughter of Aaron Moore and Mary Hollingsworth. From this union nine children were born.

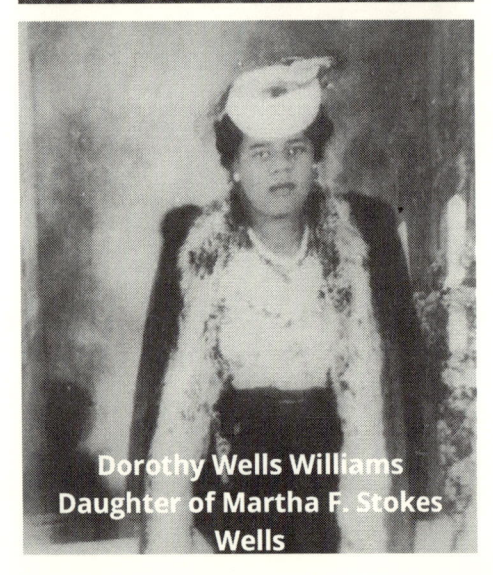

Martha F. Stokes Wells

Mary Stokes Carlton

**Dorothy Wells Williams
Daughter of Martha F. Stokes Wells**

Mary Stokes & Henry T. Carlton
1897 - 1970

Sara Stokes & John A. Wells
June 10, 1898 - November 28, 1983

James Mayso Stokes & Truie Wells
May 8, 1900 - March 10, 1980

David Matthew Stokes
November 26, 1903 - December 6, 1953

Annie B. Stokes & Enoch Southerland
August 10, 1904 - May 26, 1983

Bertha Lurena Stokes & Leroy White
June 3, 1909 - February 1987

Martha F. Stokes & Obid Adja Wells
November 27, 1909 - May 17, 1959

Sylvia Stokes
1909

Sidney Lewis Stokes & Josephine McNeill, Maxine
August 21, 1914 - March 1985

Lott Neal Murray was born in February of 1859 and he died November 26, 1933. He is the son of James Murray and Silva Simpson. He married Rosanna V. Robinson. She was born in November of 1873 and she died July 13, 1931. She is the daughter of Martin and Sarah Robinson. From this union eight children were born.

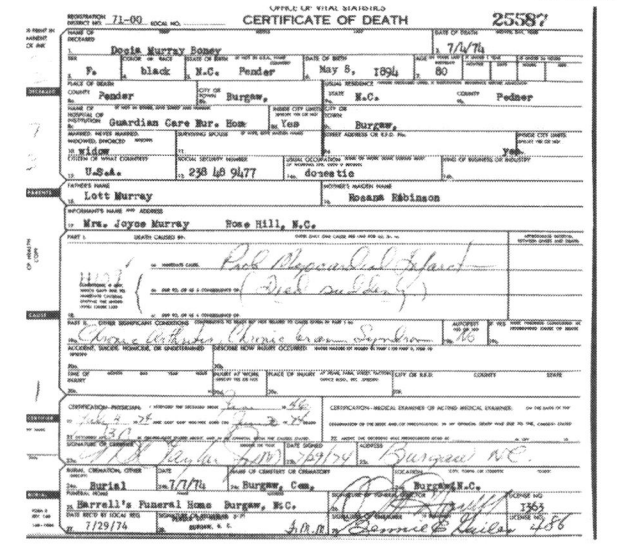

Docia Murray & James D. Boney
1894 - 1974

Sarah Murray & Oscar McMillan &
Luther Carroll
May 1897

Orrie B. Murray & Mary P. Davis
1900 - September 5, 1965

Ulysses Stephen Murray & Joyce Dixon
January 13, 1899 - March 16, 1966

Hattie Murray & Robert Burnett, Dalls Herring
April 17, 1904 - July 2, 1960

Fannie D. Murray Matthews
July 10, 1906 - April 15, 2008

Susan Gretchen Murray
1906

Lottie Viola Murray

Ulysses Stephen Murray

Joyce Dixon Murray
Wife of Ulysses Steven Murray

Roscoe Pickett was born June 30, 1887 and he died September 27, 1962 in Duplin County, North Carolina. He is the son of Albert L. Pickett and Chelsey Kenan. He married Anna Belle Newkirk. She was born in December of 1888 and she died July 2, 1957. She is the daughter of Haywood Pickett and Phoebe Kenan. From this union fourteen children were born.

Graham Carroll Pickett & Lillie Bell Powers
November 12, 1908 - December 14, 1970

Katie Pickett
1911 - 1918

Kinnie Bertha Irene Pickett & William Crawley
November 21, 1911 - August 5, 2005

Joe Hatten Pickett & Mary Blanche Judge
December 15, 1913 - September 13, 1982

Retha Bell Pickett & Elijah N. Donaldson
May 4, 1916 - May 20, 1994

Annie Ruth Pickett
August 22, 1918 - April 26, 1919

William Haywood Pickett & Harriett Newkirk
August 22, 1918 - June 3, 1989

James Roscoe Pickett & Mary Lou Graham
1920 - March 10, 2002

Ralph Hemo Pickett & Annie Murray Henderson
1922 - 1999

Mary Gladys Pickett
February 15, 1923 - August 19, 1956

Rayfield Robert Pickett
1923 - March 10, 1942

Norwood Pickett Willie Rose Farrior
March 25, 1925 - June 5, 1975

Galler Pickett
September 5, 1926 - December 26, 1926

Edna Earl Pickett
April 15, 1929 - February 7, 2007

Kinnie Bertha Pickett Crawley

William Haywood Pickett

James Roscoe Pickett

Adam J. Carlton was born in January of 1846 and he died December 26, 1931. He married Mahalia Boyette. She was born in 1857 and she died January 2, 1929. She is the daughter of Balaam Boyette and Patsy McLammy. From this union nine children were born.

James Carlton. & Effie Blount
1870

Owen B. Carlton
1973

Matthew L. Carlton
1878 - February 23, 1920

Perry F. Carlton
1879 - March 2, 1944

Ida Isabelle Carlton & Dennis Watford
February 21, 1900 - March 28, 1959

Celia Carlton & McLane Holmes
1885 - January 29, 1926

Rev. Utley Adam Carlton & Alberta Sampson
April 4, 1887 - May 18, 1963

John Carlton & Effie Blount
1889

Leander Carlton
1896 - 1964

Balam Gavin was born in 1854 and no death date was found on him. He is the son of Amy Gavin. He married Julia Ann Smith on June 25, 1885 in Duplin County, North Carolina. She was born January 15, 1995 in Duplin County, North Carolina. She is the daughter of Aaron & Lucy Smith. She was born October 22, 1854 and she died March 27, 1950. From this union eleven children were born.

Alphia Gavin & Will Frederick
November 20, 1884 - October 23, 1949

Estell Gavin
1892

Luther H. Gavin
June 27, 1894 - September 23, 1962

Nettie Gavin & Manuel Bryant
November 26, 1896 - June 5, 1981

Pearl Gavin & Samuel Chaetam
1895

Covious Gavin
May 10, 1896 - December 1915

Corrina Gavin
1896

Mittie Gavin Mitchell
November 26, 1898 - December 1, 1990

Lenora Gavin
September 4, 1911 - November 11, 1950

Frederick Gavin
1905

James Manley Gavin
May 24, 1906 - September 7, 1978

76

Jefferson Davis Miller was born May 4, 1861 and he died February 11, 1940. He is the son of Jack Miller and Sarah McIver. He married Sarah Ann Jarmon. She was born in 1872 and no death date was found on her. From this union thirteen children were born.

Mozilla Miller & Hinton Smith
1886 - January 21, 1934

Freeman Green Miller & Mary Southerland
May 26, 1889 - March 8, 1981

Hattie E. Miller
October 13, 1892 - June 12, 1924

William Curtis Miller & Mary Prudance Hargrove
January 26, 1896 - May 6, 1960

Carrie J. Miller
1895

Maggie Ivy Miller
February 28, 1900 - March 13, 1965

Sarah Miller
1900

Eliza Miller
1901

Annie Miller Pendargrass
1904 - April 30, 2006

Katie Mille & Rufus Middleton
1906

John Albert Millier
March 4, 1906 - December 16, 1974

Nettie Mae Miller
April 13, 1910 - October 26, 2005

Lillie Belle Miller & Leroy Newborn
1915

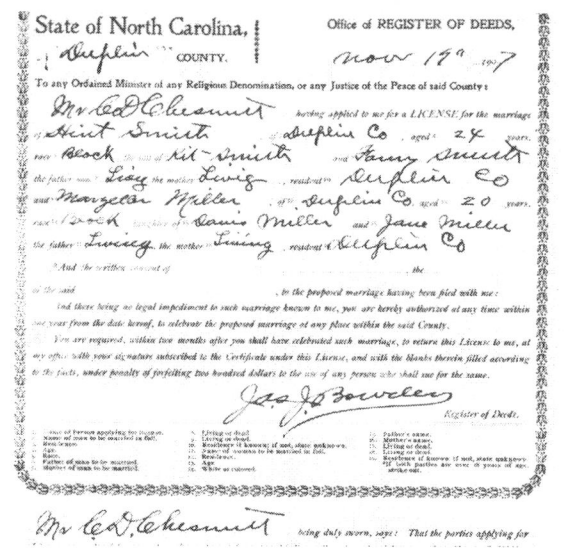

Phoebe Rhodes was born in 1842 and she died March 13, 1921 in Warsaw, Duplin County, North Carolina. She married Jim Southerland. From this union seven children were born.

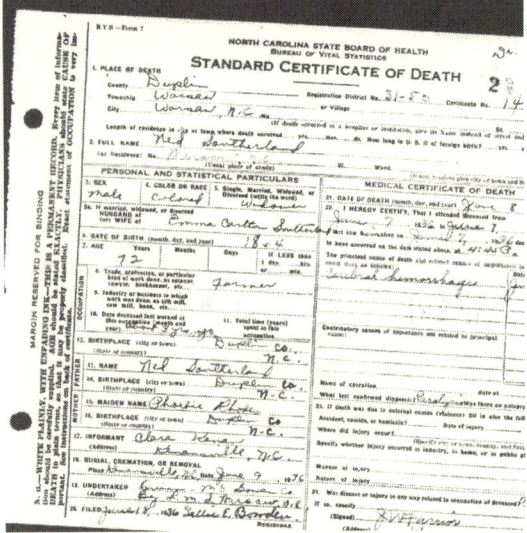

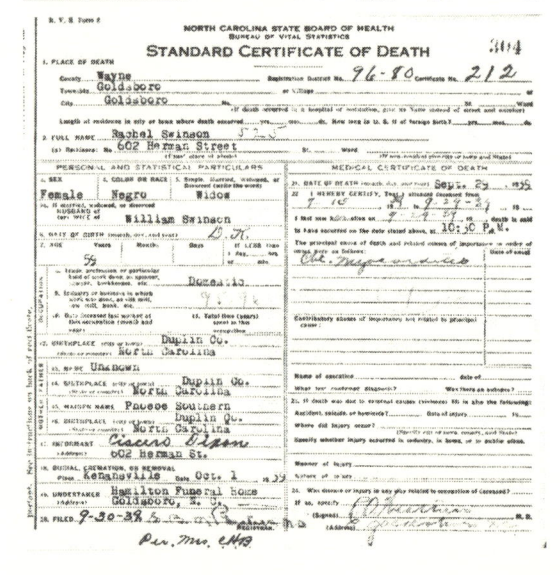

Joe Southerland & Susan Sandlin
February 9, 1858 - March 12, 1935

Ned Southerland & Emma Carlton
Feb 1864 - June 8, 1936

Sarah D. Southerland
1868

Chelsy Southerland & Matthew Pearsall
1873 - December 31, 1949

Rachel M. Southerland & William Swinson
1880 - September 29, 1939

Mary J. Southerland
1877

Martha Southerland
1878

78

Mayo Outlaw was born in 1860 and he died May 30, 1936. He is the son of Absalom Outlaw and Charity Davis. He married Hannah Jarman. She was born in 1855 and no death date was found on her. She is the daughter of Cassie Jarmon. From this union fifteen children were born.

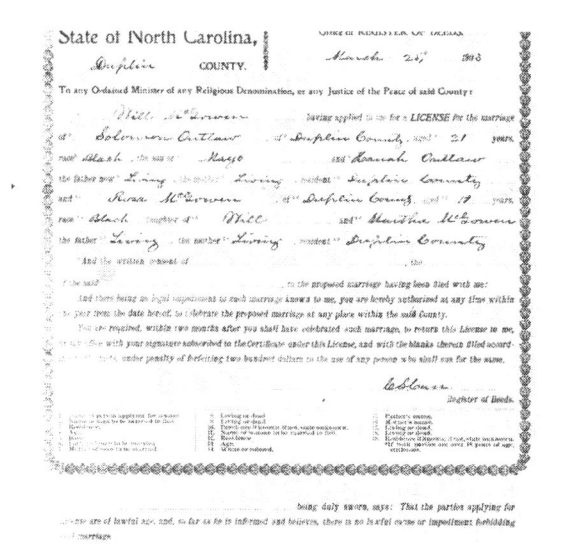

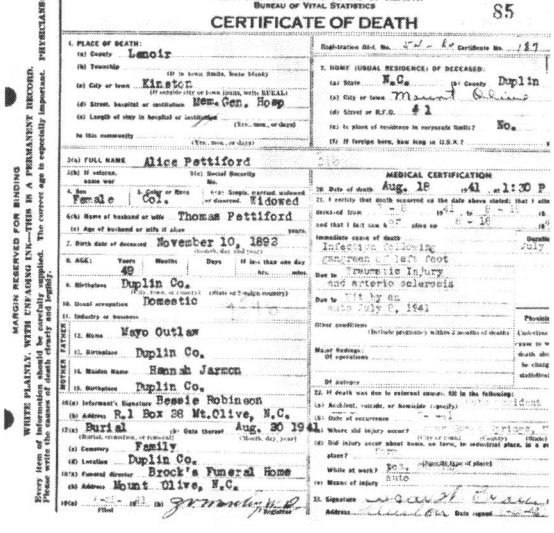

Idella Outlaw & Frank Branch
1872

Edmond Outlaw
1874

Cornelius Outlaw
1875

William A. Outlaw & Roberta Freeman
1876

Charity Outlaw
1878

Peter Outlaw & Sophie Jarman, Lucy Miller
March 1879

Soloman Outlaw & Rosa McGowan
1882

Hosea Outlaw & Mary Jane Dixon
January 31, 1883 - March 25, 1965

Mattie Outlaw & Richard Branch
February 1884 - November 16, 1951

Charity Outlaw
1888

Estella Outlaw & Kit Smith
1890

Alice Outlaw & Thomas Pettiford
November 10, 1892 - August 18, 1941

Callie Outlaw
1896

Mayo Elmore Outlaw & Lizzie Jones
February 13, 1893 - April 21, 1958

Leonard Outlaw
1917

Henry Clay McGowan was born February 10, 1861 and he died September 15, 1940 in Kenansville, Duplin County, North Carolina. He is the son of George A. McGowan and Lucy Jane Stokes. He married Annie Pearsall. She was born in December of 1862 and she died November 28, 1915. From this union nine children were born.

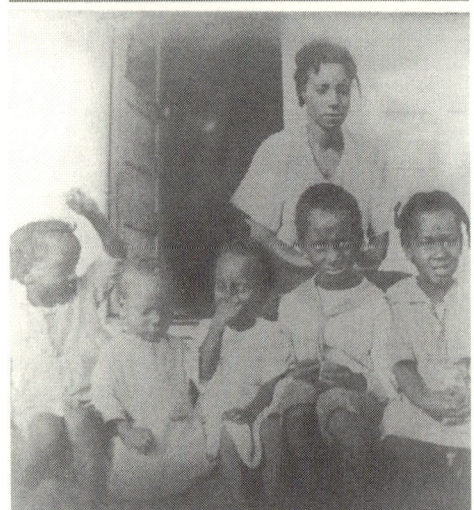

Martha McGowan & Oscar Smith
September 24, 1886 - April 12, 1949

Lucy McGowan & Jim James Jarmon
May 22, 1888 - November 17, 1948

George McGowan & Sarah Kenan
July 17, 1890 - May 5, 1970

Emma McGowan
1893

Lawrence McGowan
1895

Florence McGowan & Arthur Bradshaw
February 10, 1895 - April 24, 1950

Sula Bell McGowan & John C. McGee
July 31, 1897 - May 16, 1963

Henry Ned McGowan & Martha A. Miller
December 27, 1899 - March 9, 1951

Cornelia McGowan & Henry G. Outlaw
April 20, 1907 - July 15, 1942

80

James Madison Hall was born August 1, 1850 and he died August 18, 1904 in Magnolia, Duplin County, North Carolina. He is the son of Dennis and Hannah Hall. He married Harriett J. Bryant. She was born August 25, 1855 and she died November 17, 1937 in Magnolia, Duplin County, North Carolina. She is the daughter of Benjamin & Delsie Bryant. From this union eight children were born.

Benjamin Adolphus Hall
November 28, 1876 - August 27, 1940

Preston Hall
1879- 1891

James Burse Hall
July 1, 1880 - April 1956

Minnie Hall & George Dixon
March 31, 1889 - May 12, 1969

Ada L. Hall & Edward Hall
October 1, 1888 - May 17, 1952

Dennis Lee Hall Sr. & Cornelia Southerland
January 12, 1892 - February 15, 1961

Lue Ella Hall
January 24, 1894 - February 17, 1975

John Livingston Hall
September 26, 1896 - June 23, 1984

Rev. Joseph Henry Lowe was born February 14, 1876 and he died December 15, 1955 in Warsaw, Duplin County, North Carolina. He is the son of Jim D. Lowe and Eliza Bowden. He married Annie Amelia Miller March 7, 1900 in Duplin County, North Carolina. She was born in 1881 and she died June 29, 1955. She is the daughter of Clabourne Miller Sr. and Sarah McIver From this union twelve children were born.

Joseph Lowe

Clabon Lowe

Henry Lee Lowe

Rev. Sarah Liza Lowe Hamilton
1901 - 1978

James Council Lowe
1903 - 1920

Henry Lee Lowe & Lillie Newkirk
July 15, 1904 - November 7, 1992

Lillie Belle Lowe & Jimmy Russell McCallop
May 20, 1907 - April 16, 1983

Joseph Lowe . & Louise Kenan
May 12, 1909 - April 27, 1981

Julia Ellen Lowe
October 5, 1910 - January 15, 1990

James Edward Lowe Sr. & Alice Gavin
July 16, 1911 - June 23, 1960

Annie Lucille Lowe & Marshall Bouyer
April 7, 1913 - November 14, 2001

Claybon Lowe & Clara Bostic
June 14, 1915 - September 1, 1997

Limon Wouten Lowe Sr. & Mary Lillie Newton
July 30, 1918 - June 24, 1991

Sallie Lee Lowe & William Elijah Cooper
April 29, 1921 - May 10, 2011

Levi Montee Lowe Sr. & Mabel Faison
February 23, 1925 - September 9, 2011

Henry Branch was born in August of 1843 and he died February 6, 1927 in Duplin County, North Carolina. He is the son of Garrison Branch and Dilsey Hussey. He married Rebecca Jane Outlaw. She was born in 1850 and she died August 24, 1924. She is the daughter of Absalom and Charity Outlaw. From this union thirteen children were born.

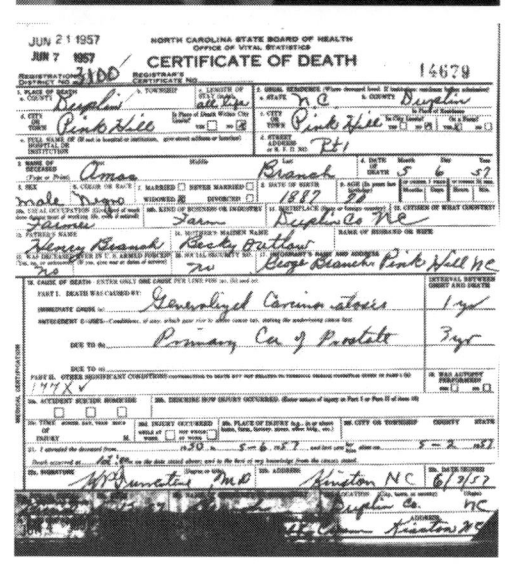

Frank David Branch & Della Outlaw
1868 - December 6, 1952

Edith Branch & Everett Graham
October 16, 1872 - October 19, 1965

General Grant Branch
1872

William H. Branch & Katy Stroud
August 10, 1889 - June 11, 1951

Angeline Branch
1875

Martha J. Branch & Jonah Outlaw
1877

Richard Branch & Minnie Locks
1880

Princes Branch & Ben Stanley
October 14, 1883 - March 8, 1972

Lou Branch & Larry Smith
April 21, 1886 - October 1970

Gaston Branch & Minnie Smith, Hannah Stroud
May 19, 1886 - December 3, 1960

Amos Branch & Katie Grady
June 25, 1887 - May 6, 1957

Lilly Branch & Alonzo Miller
March 18, 1891 - August 23, 1928

Richard Branch & Mattie Outlaw
January 15, 1893 - September 5, 1970

83

Harry Farrior was born in 1847 and he died June 25, 1917 Kenansville, North Carolina. He married Mary Pearsall on February 20, 1879 in Duplin County, North Carolina. She was born in 1860 and no death date was found on her. From this union thirteen children were born.

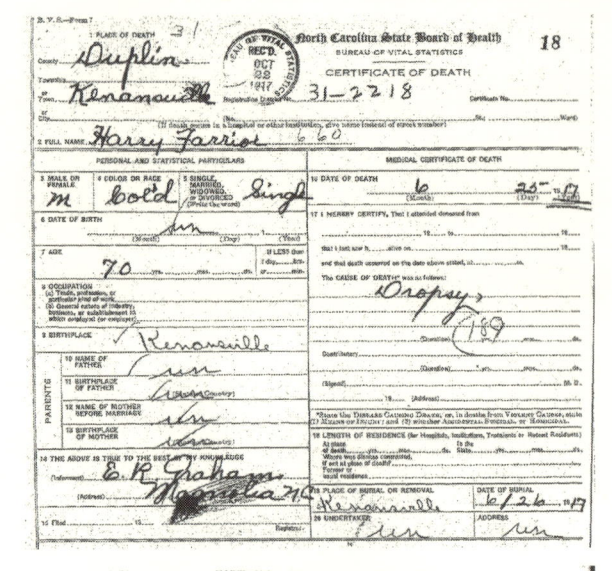

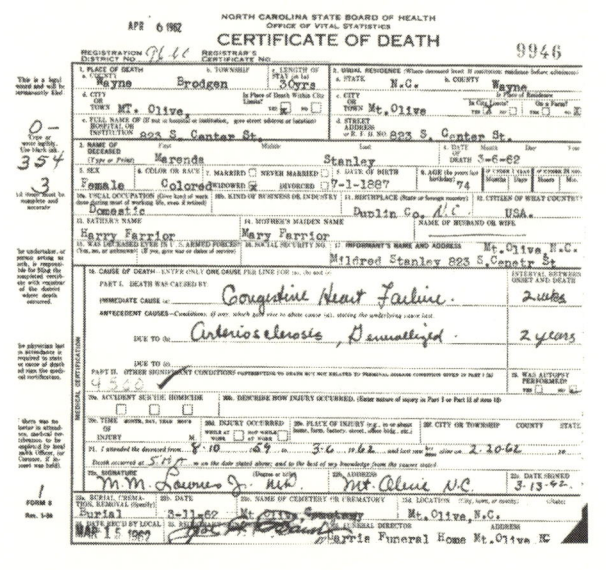

Lizzie Farrior
1867

George Farrior
1868

Nick Farrior
1871

Willie Farrior & Hattie Herring
1873

Anna Farrior & James Arthur Cockerham
August 16, 1889 - November 16, 1929

Marenda Farrior & George Stanley
July 1, 1887 - March 6, 1962

John Farrior
1885

Harry Bell Farrior & Sudie Southerland
1889 - July 12, 1928

Benjamin Farrior & Minnie Lewis
1891

Clarence J. Farrior & Annie Powell
October 15, 1888 - November 14, 1961

Emma Farrior
1893

Albert and Mary Farrior
January 12, 1898 - March 12, 1971

William Farrior & Hattie Herring
February 28, 1900 - September 29, 1985

Alonzo Franklin Miller was born in 1875 and he died July 20, 1936. He married Mittie Outlaw January 5, 1914 in Duplin County, North Carolina. She was born in 1895 and no death date was found on her. She is the daughter of Isaac and Mary M. Grady Outlaw. From this union twelve children were born.

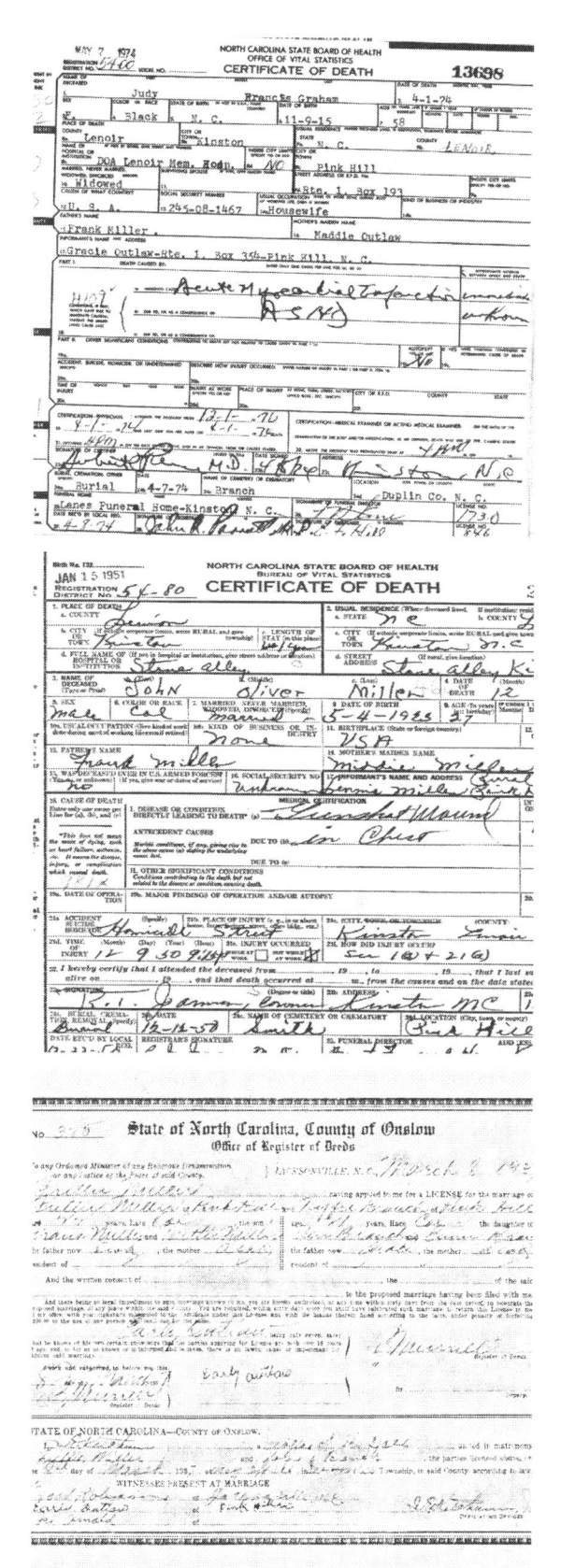

Lennie Miller & Mildred Newborn
May 22, 1911 - October 5, 1984

Freely Miller & Nessie Branch
August 23, 1914 - April 22, 1996

Judy Frances Miller & James Graham
November 9, 1915 - April 1, 1974

Mary Miller Miles
1916 - February 14, 1939

Mack Miller
September 1918

Lucy Miller
1919

Janie Miller
July 31, 1921 - July 31, 1941

John Oliver Miller & Alzona Payton
May 4, 1923 - December 9, 1950

Leatha Mae Miller
Feb 6, 1926

Elouise Miller
1925

Charlie Raymond Miller
October 13, 1928 - August 4, 1995

Minnie Ruth Miller
1929

Tom Fennell was Born August 1, 1880 and he died March 5, 1924. He is the son of Perry and Lydia Fennell. He married Mary Rosa Murphy. She was born in 1873 and she died Died December 18, 1928. She is the daughter of Stanford Anderson Murphy and Julia Ann Foster (Fox). From this union six children were born.

Mary M. Fennell
1898

William Henry Fennell & Sadie Gray
1904

Alice Fennell & John James Teachey
July 11, 1907 - May 24, 1996

Leddie Virginia Fennell & Obbie Boykin
March 24, 1908 - May 3, 1972

Julia Fennell
1911

Janie Bernice Fennell & Willie Faison
1914 - 1965

86

Peter Wallace was born in 1852 and no death was found on him. He married Penelope Herring. She was born in 1856 and no death date date was found on here. From this union ten children were born.

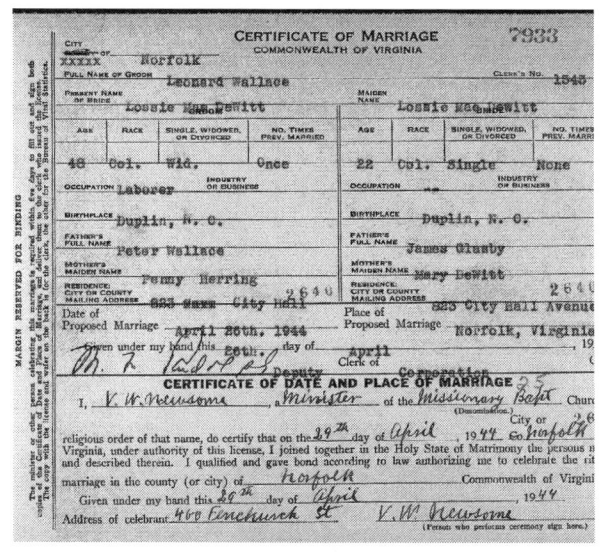

Saphronia Wallace & John Grady
1874

Annie Wallace Dobson
1875 - October 25, 1936

Minnie Wallace
1879 - December 22, 1945

Olive Wallace
June 4, 1883

Chelly Wallace
1885

Leonard Wallace & Katie Moore
May 31, 1889 - November 22, 1964

Lillie Wallace & Isaac Christopher Frederick
November 23, 1891 - November 26, 1941

William Wallace & Elnora Wallace
1895 - January 16, 1965

Pearl Lee Wallace & Emerson Wesley Wiliams
April 23, 1900 - December 12, 1986

James Eddie Wallace & Thelma
February 18, 1901 - December 14, 1961

87

Elder Banks Alderman was born March 18, 1866 and no death date was found on him. He is the son of Robert Sherman Alderman and Rachel Ann Graham. He married Hannah Surrene Moore. She was born August 17, 1871 and she died October 5, 1938. She is the daughter of Aaron Moore and Mary Hollingsworth. From this union nine children were born.

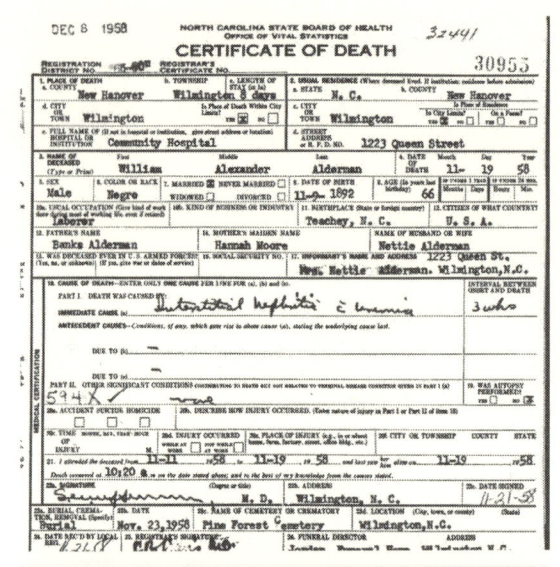

William Alexander Alderman & Nettie Campbell
November 9, 1892 - November 19, 1958

Mary Rachel Alderman & McDuffie Newkirk
January 1, 1895 - April 14, 1968

Banks Ined Alderman & Clara Barden
September 7, 1897 - January 2, 1936

Robert Aaron Alderman (James Brown)
June 27, 1899 - May 29, 1983

Elder Mitchell Alderman
June 20, 1902 - June 22, 1988

Doctor Benjamin Alderman & Annie Louise Highsmith
April 12, 1904 - July 6, 1993

Martha C. Alderman & Isaac Keith
1906 - 1988

Archie Alderman
1910

Hattie Marie Alderman & Bishop John Clifton
May 10, 1910 - June 25, 2000

James Leakes Wells was born in 1876 and no death date was found on him. He is the son of Jerry and Matilda Wells. He married Mary Laura Murphy on July 15, 1897 in Duplin County, North Carolina. From this union six children were born.

Lula A. Wells and Matthew John Southerland.
May 30, 1898 - September 4, 1974

Mary W. Wells & Harry L. Huggins
February 27, 1899 - November 1982

Bertha Wells & Edward D. Powers
April 17, 1900 - January 26, 1956

Nellie H. Wells & Robert Leslie Boney
September 1, 1903 - February 24, 1972

Liston Wells & Lillie Williams
1906

John Henry Wells & Carrie Stringfield
March 21, 1907 - October 1, 1961

Garlie Chasten was born November 21, 1893 and he died January 21, 1976. He is the son of Susan Chasten. He married Katie Dixon. She was born in 1901 and she died August 16, 1925. She is the daughter of Abram Dixon and Lucy Ann Graham. From this union seven children were born. Garlie later married Addie Boney. She was born February 15, 1894 and she died October 24, 1944. She is the daughter of John Thomas Boney and Julia Pearsall.

Garlie Chasten Sr.

Leroy Chasten

Garlie Chasten Jr.

1st Wife Katie Dixon's children

Venette Chasten & Johnie R. Carr
1923 - April 21, 2009

Jessie Leroy Chasten & Mattie Delois Murray
July 1, 1924 - February 17, 2007

2nd wife Abigail Boney Herring's children

Margaret Chasten
January 4, 1931 - July 17, 1978

Elnora Chasten
January 15, 1934 - April 24, 1954

Garlie W. Chasten Jr.
April 19, 1935 - August 1, 2004

Henry J. Matthews was born June 10, 1866 and he died August 6, 1955 in Duplin County, North Carolina. He is the son of Fleet C. Matthews and Louise Hussey. He married Catherine Chasten August 30, 1888 in Duplin County, North Carolina. She was born May 2, 1854 and she died August 3, 1917 in Island Creek, Duplin County, North Carolina. She is the daughter of Isaac Chasten and Susan (Hollingsworth) Kilpatrick. From this union Eleven children were born.

John Henry Matthews & Mittie Faison
1882

Mamie Matthis & James Carr
January 1884 - 1911

Mary Matthes
1885

Lummie Matthews & Christopher Columbus Murray
November 7, 1891 - May 11, 1963

Early Lloyd Matthews & Mamie Lula Carr
March 18, 1894 - May 27, 1966

Lillian D. Matthews
1894

James Pearlie Matthews & Bettie Williams
July 13, 1896 - May 15, 1939

Bud Mathews
1897

Hallie Matthews & Alice Southerland
February 5, 1898

Collete Matthis & Cicero Dobson Sr.
January 31, 1901 - March 20, 1935

Isaac Wilbert Matthews
1907

Thomas Henry Chasten was born in 1876 and he died May 2, 1941 in Beaulaville, Duplin County, North Carolina. He is the son of Lott Chasten and Molet Brown. He married Ida Jane Jones March 20, 1901 in Duplin County, North Carolina. She was born January 27, 1881 and she died May 2, 1952 in Kinston, Lenoir County, North Carolina. She is the daughter of John Henry Jones and Leah J Hall. From this union seven children were born.

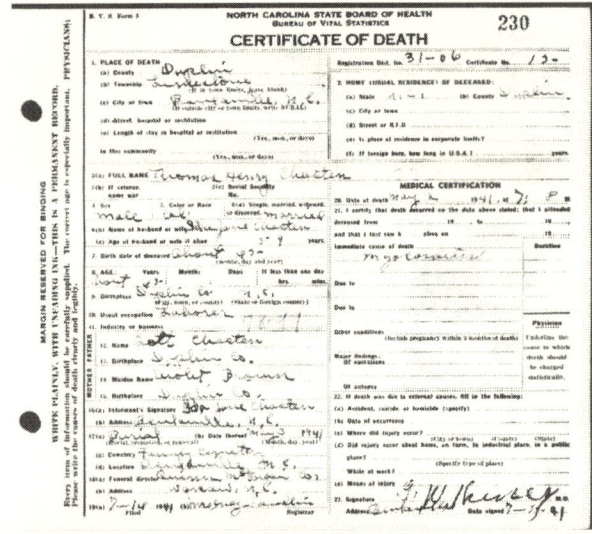

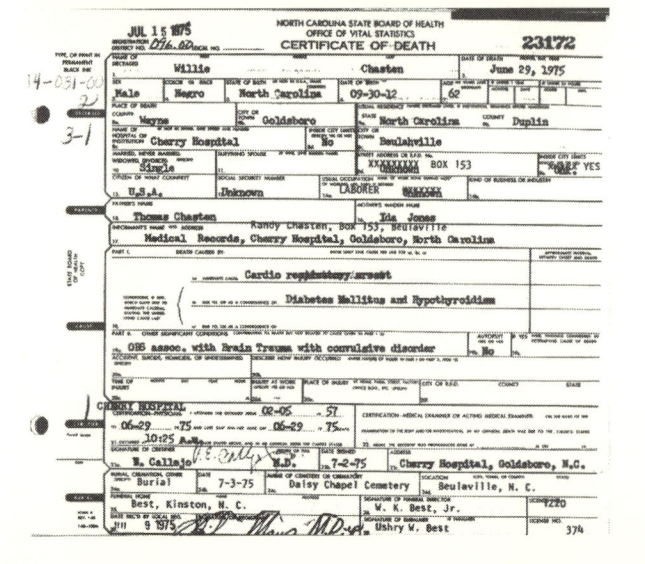

McKinley Chasten
March 4, 1903 - April 13, 1928

James C. Chasten and Mary A. McMillan
April 15, 1904 - May 17, 1981

Norman Chasten and Jonie L. Davis
March 6, 1909 - September 9, 1984

Willie Chasten
September 30, 1912 - June 19, 1975

Ransom Chasten
June 7, 1914 - October 26, 1995

Thomas Henry Chance Jr. & Maggie Mae Parker
November 14, 1917 - June 29, 1986

Ida Mildred Chasten
May 25, 1919 - June 19, 1993

Henry Judge was born May 10, 1869 and he died September 8, 1933 in Cypress Creek, Duplin County, North Carolina. He is the son of Moses Judge and Katheryn Pickett. He married Carrie Kelly. She was born in 1884 and she died February 10, 1942 in Duplin County, North Carolina. She is the daughter of Allen Kelly and Louisa Murray. From this union eleven children were born.

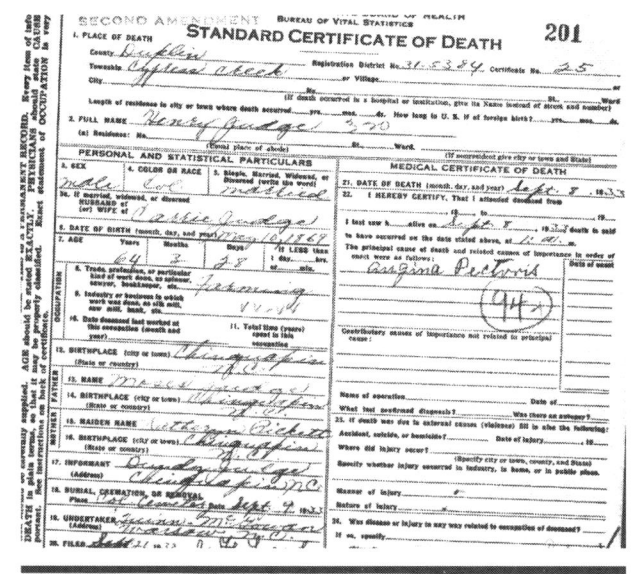

Leslie James Judge & Vassie Whitehead
1895

Rosella Judge & Richard Graham
June 10, 1898 - July 19, 1921

Lonnie P. Judge Sr. & Hattie Turner
September 16, 1899 - October 28, 1963

Hattie Florence Judge & George Robert Hill
August 1, 1902 - August 29, 1966

Opie Roosevelt Judge
April 7, 1904 - May 23, 1965

Stedman T. Judge & Loula Andry Hall
December 23, 1903 - December 30, 1966

Fuller Odell Judge & Mary Frances Jones
1908 - March 23, 1937

Katie Judge
December 18, 1910 - December 8, 1921

Rosella Judge
1910

Dudley Gleamon Judge & Agnes Lawrence
June 16, 1914 - September 29, 1974

Mattie Judge
1917

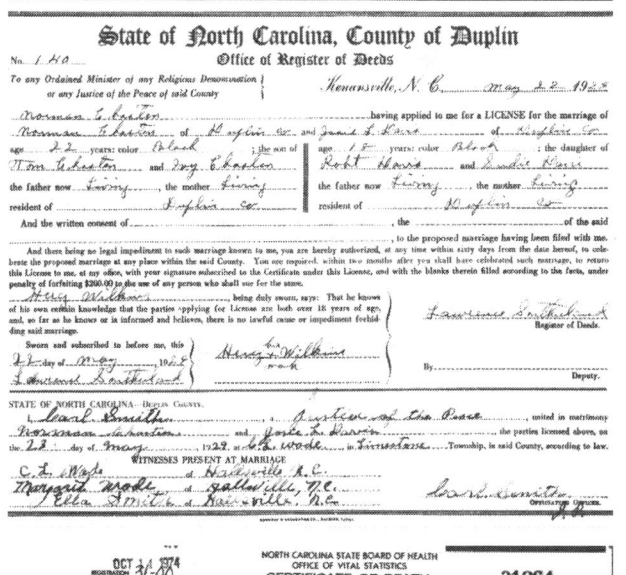

William Robinson (Roberson) was born in 1841 and no death date was found on him. He married Hannah Wallace. She was born in 1853 and she died October 18, 1939. She is the daughter of Sylvia Wallace. From this union seventeen children were born.

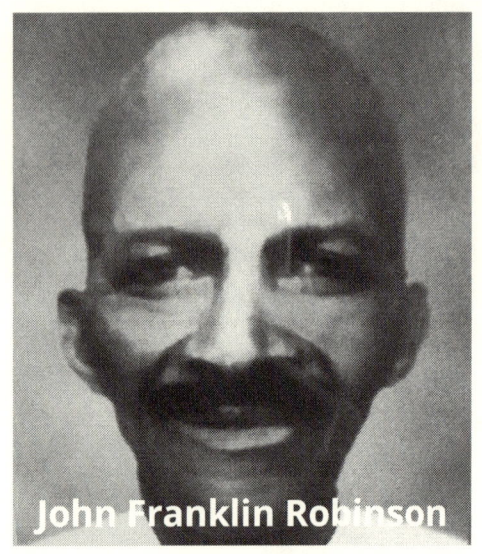

John Franklin Robinson

Ella Precilla Bowden Robinson

Hattie Adell Robinson Ammons

Willie Robinson
1872

Ellen Robinson & Robert Solice
September 1, 1873 - 1953

Henry Robison
May 1875 - April 19, 1953

John Franklin Robinson & Precilla Bowden
1880 - July 17, 1950

Billie Robinson
1884

Lonnie Robinson
August 15, 1884 - July 2, 1920

Glennie Robinson
1886 - December 25, 1931

Lizzie Robinson & Freddie Garner
August 15, 1889 - August 24, 1980

Bertha & Robert Bowden
July 19, 1890 - October 11, 1918

Cora Robinson
1891 - December 22, 1973

Lonnie & Annie Ratliff
1897 - July 2, 197

Estella & Alexander McKinney
Juney 30, 1897 - September 1, 1997

Walter Robinson
May 10, 1898 - December 9, 1953

Mamie Robinson & Lafayette Jones
February 27, 1899 - July 16, 1973

Finnie Robinson
November 15, 1905 - October 2, 1975

Bessie Robinson & Clarence Jones
May 15, 1905 - September 1, 1997

Essie Robinson Branch
December 3, 1911 - December 4, 1964

Julia Stokes was born in March of 1872 and she died March 25, 1933 in Chinquapin, Duplin County, North Carolina. She is the daughter of Scott Stokes and Edna Whitfield. She married Silas Pickett on June 28, 1891 in Duplin County, North Carolina. He was born June 21, 1865 and he died February 8, 1940 in Chiquapin, Duplin County, North Carolina. He is the son of Friday Pickett and Marinda Becton. From this union eleven children were born.

Christopher Columbus Pickett

Thurman Emanuel Pickett

Willie Arthur Murray Sr.

Emma Pickett
November 20, 1889 - September 20, 1949

Dundy Pickett & Louvenia Rochelle
March 29, 1891 - March 5, 1977

James Douglass Pickett & Sarah Carr
January 22, 1892 - April 24, 1968

Edith Frances Pickett
June 19, 1894 - February 26, 1971

Neady Viola Pcikett
June 26, 1895 - December 29, 1977

Willie Scott Pickett
September 7, 1897 - January 20, 1983

Alonza Chestnut Pickett
October 1898 - November 14, 1977

Stanley McKinley Pickett
February 28, 1901 - October 28, 1972

Roosevelt Washington Pickett & Eliza Jane Lee
October 13, 1902 - February 12, 2019

Bessie Adley Pickett
July 19, 1905 - April 8, 1891

Lillie S. Pickett
1907 - March 24, 1967

Daniel J. Carlton was born in 1869 and he died December 16, 1929 in Faison, Duplin County, North Carolina. He is the son of Alfred and Caroline Carlton. He married Martha Carlton. She was born July 13, 1869 and she died July 1, 1952 in Wayne County, North Carolina. She is the daughter of Calvin Carlton and Lucy Frederick. Form this union eight children were born.

Mary Carlton
1893

James Hedrick Carlton & Minnie Boykin

Katie Bell Carlton & William Henry Pearsall
July 13, 1896 - July 1, 1952

Willie Calvin Carlton
April 1, 1889 - October 15, 1975

George Daniel Carlton & Ethel King
October 22, 1899 - February 1978

Eure A. Carlton & Annie Bass
1902

Lucy C. Carlton & Glasco King
1904

John Carlton & Lola Wallace
August 7, 1902 - November 16, 1969

Louis M. Cooper was born May 29, 1889 and he died June 13, 1938 in Kenansville, Duplin County, North Carolina. He is the son of Moses Cooper and Martha Monk. He married Emma Kenan. She was born May 12, 1886 and she died April 18, 1956 in Kennansville, Duplin County, North Carolina. She is the daughter of Tony Kenan and Julia Hussey. From this union twelve children were born.

Albert Cooper & Marie Murray
August 17, 1905 - March 21, 1964

Anna Elizabeth Cooper & Earl Lafayette Pickett Sr.
March 12, 1905 - August 21, 1985

Hattie Cooper & George Luther Middleton Jr.
June 15, 1910 - October 7, 1971

Tony Cooper Jr. & Laura Washington
March 22, 1914 - March 23, 1961

Polly Cooper Williams
June 6, 1915 - June 8, 1988

Louise Cooper Jr. & Catherine Everett
July 23, 1918

Herman Cooper
March 25, 1922 - July 5, 1967

Roy Cooper
January 21, 1923 - January 29, 1923

Catherine Cooper & Robert E. Jones
September 21, 1926 - February 15, 2019

Mathew Cooper & Bessie Lee Middleton
April 15, 1927 - February 9, 1964

Sarah Dixon was born October 24, 1866 and she died August 6, 1918 in Duplin County, North Carolina. She is the daughter of Samuel Dixon and Hannah Farrior. She married Arnold Murray. He was born in May of 1856 and no death date was found on him. He is the son of Jack and Lavinia Teachy Murray. From this union eight children were born.

Johnnie Elijah Murray & Sarah Catherine Register
October 28, 1885

Vinie Murray
1888

Christopher Columbus Murray & Lummie Matthews
April 27, 1890 - August 5, 1964

Council & Blanchie Murray
1892 - February 2, 1919

Samuel J. Murray & Hattie C. Gibbs Bryant
October 17, 1892 - November 12, 1976

William James Murray
June 27, 1896 - December 11, 1951

Rachel Murray & John Lanier
July 5, 1897 - September 3, 1942

Margaret J. Murray & Liston Judge
August 1899 - February 25, 1972

Joseph Hall was born in 1866 and he died December 3, 1937. He is the son of Dennis and Hannah Hall. He married Caroline Southerland. She was born in January of 1870 and she died March 14, 1950 in Rose Hill, Duplin County, North Carolina. She is the daughter of Martin Southerland and Harriett Parrish. From this union seven children were born.

James Napthian Hall & Ada Jacobs
December 1, 1897 - August 1974

Lou Della Hall & William H. Robinson
Novmebr 1, 1899 - September 3, 1989

Owen Wright Hall & Maggie Herring, Gertrude Williams
October 16, 1901 - March 4, 1987

Hettie Belle Hall & Milton King
February 2, 1901 - January 22, 1992

Joseph Tim Hall & Julia Ann Corbett
December 23, 1903 - April 23, 1962

Calvin Hall
April 15, 1910 - October 14, 1979

Luther Mae Hall & Jeremiah Herring
March 19, 1912 - April 21, 1996

Ralph B. Hall

Mansfield Allen Newkirk was born January 17, 1841 and he died December 26, 1895 in Duplin County, North Carolina. He married Charity Rollins January 25, 1868 in Duplin County, North Carolina. She was born in 1840 and no death date was found on her. She is the daughter of Rebecca Rollins. From this union seven children were born.

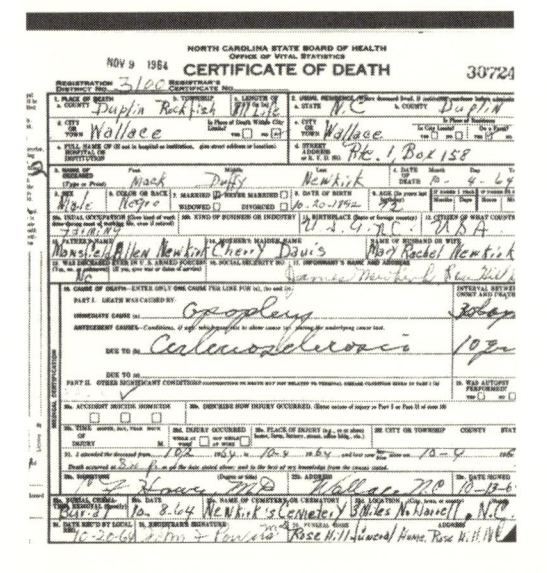

Alice Newkirk Faison

Nancy Ellen Newkirk & Robert Lee Peterson
August 1870 - May 21, 1927

Rachel A. Newkirk
1871

James Malachi Newkirk
January 17, 1875 - May 18, 1967

Alice N. Newkirk & John M. Faison
July 15, 1878 - October 23, 1961

John T. Newkirk & Fannie Moore
December 1881

Mary S. Newkirk & Edward Fauklner
July 27, 1881

McDuffie Newkirk & Mary Rachel Alderman
October 1892 - October 4, 1964

100

Isaac Outlaw was born in 1847 and he died January 27, 1922 in New Hanover County, North Carolina. He married Julia Smith. She was born in 1860 and no death date was found on her. He later married Mary Susan Grady February 14, 1896 in Duplin County, North Carolina. She was born in 1850 and she died February 21, 1937. She is the daughter of Alex and Zilphia Grady.

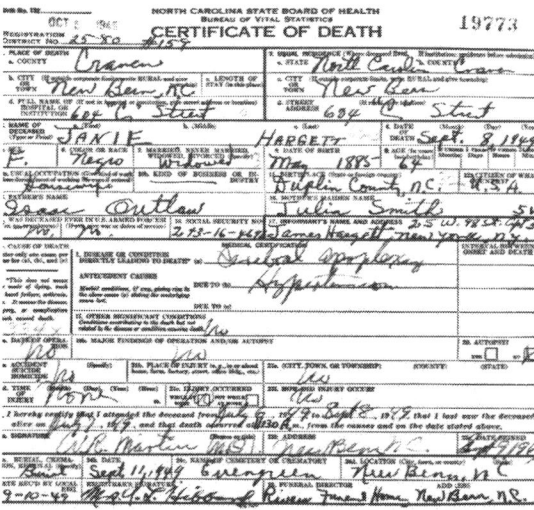

Robert Outlaw and Maggie Loftin
1872

Annie Outlaw
1873

Malvina Outlaw & Columbus George
1877 - November 19, 1952

Janie Outlaw & George Allen Hargett
May 1885 - September 8, 1948

101

Charles Kenan was born in 1830 and no death date was found on him. He married Charlotte "Charity" Graham. She was born in February of 1835 and she died November 8, 1914 in Duplin County, North Carolina. She is the daughter of Lewis Graham. From this union twelve children were born.

Richard Kenan & Hannah G. Batts
August 27, 1854 - March 31, 1941

Charlie Henry & Mollie Kenan
January 15, 1856 - May 13, 1945

George Kenan & Margianna Williams
1858

Joseph Kenan
1861

Mariah Kenan
1863

Fred Kenan
1865

Lewis Kenan & Lucy Barden
1865

Grant Kenan
1866

Chelsey Kenan & Albert L. Pickett
May 1866 - April 8, 1925

Sherman Kenan & Harriett Haley
1867

Hardy Kenan & Sallie Bryant
1873 - April 4, 1941

Lucy Kenan
1874

Claborne Miller Sr. was born August 6, 1852 and he died January 23, 1927 in Duplin County, North Carolina. He is the son of Jack Miller and Jemina Miles. He married Sarah McIver. She was born September 20, 1850 and she died February 7, 1945 in Kenansville, Duplin County, North Carolina. She is the daughter of Henry McIver and Eliza McGowan. From this union twelve children were born.

William Thomas Miller Sr. & Annie McIver
October 1875 - November 25, 1929

John Richard Miller Sr. & Emma McIver
July 12, 1875 - March 21, 1941

Tommie Miller
1875

Annie Amelia Miller & Rev. Joseph Henry Lowe
January 15, 1881 - June 29, 1955

Council & Susie Mciver
February 1884

Louisa Miller & Nelson McIver
January 1889 - December 24, 1941

Claboure Miller Jr. & Eliza Jane Smith
March 14, 1890 - March 15, 1959

Lula A. Miller Ashford
January 18, 1892 - September 7, 1966

Stephen Miller & Mary Lou Ashford
September 18, 1893 - June 5, 1965

Minnie Ann Miller & Arnold Hall
January 1894 - January 11, 1981

Davis E. Miller
1904 - 1940

Roland E. Miller
July 4, 1904 - March 1977

William Dixon was born in 1886 and he died July 11, 1961 in Hoke County, North Carolina. He is the of Jerry and Jane Dixon. He married Bessie Fussell. She was born in 1890 and she died February 26, 1971. She is the daughter of Brister Fussell and Rebecca P. Newkirk. From this union eleven children were born.

Andrew Dixon
1911

Jarvis Carlton Dixon & Irene Elizabeth Williams
November 12, 1913 - December 1989

Cleveland Dixon & Glennie Lofton
August 26, 1914 - October 12, 1991

Margaret Dixon & James Dudley Henry
September 28, 1916 - February 12, 2007

Minnie Dixon & Robert Pollock
1919

Edna Lee Dixon & Henry Ellis Sr.
May 28, 1922 - February 1991

Charlie James Dixon
January 4, 1924 - November 1, 1972

Junius Lee Dixon
August 26, 1926 - January 9, 1997

William Theodore & Sudie Mae Dixon
December 31, 1929 - December 1, 1972

Eloise Dixon
1931

Katie F. Dixon
1935

John Wesley McGowan was born April 5, 1872 and he died November 5, 1937 in Kenansville, Duplin County, North Carolina. He is the son of George Ashford McGowan and Lucy Jane Stokes. He married Melinda Miller. She was born in 1877 and she died May 6, 1928 in Kenansville, Duplin County, North Carolina. She is the daughter of Bryant Miller and Jemina McIver. From this union five children were born. John Wesley later married Henrietta Spears McIver. She is the daughter of Louis Spears and Amanda Grady. From this union five children were born.

(1st wife Melinda Miller)

Genieve Jemima McGowan & Sam Cooper
1902 - 1946

Ellie Virginia McGowan & Oby Smith
1904 - January 1, 1948

Lilly McGowan & Davis Miller
1907 - October 27, 1954

Nathan Bryant McGowan & Joanna McIver, Lucile Outlaw
January 2, 1912 - June 30, 1966

Lacy McGowan & Olivia Miller
August 26, 1915 - March 9, 1964

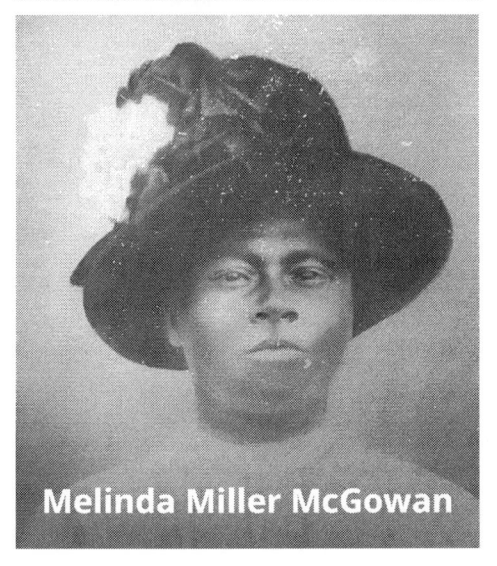

John Wesley McGowan

Nathan Bryant McGowan

Melinda Miller McGowan

James Harmon Wells was born in 1861 an no death date was found on him. He married Lucretia Farrior January 15, 1882 in Duplin County, North Carolina. She was born in 1861 and no death date was found on her. She is the daughter of Henry and Hannah Farrior. From this union eight children were born.

Louberta Wells & George Kelly
1881 - September 5, 1926

Nettie Wells & Anthony Pickett
1882 - 1June 14, 1946

Bettie Wells & James Owen Newkirk
April 15, 1886 - May 20, 1957

Armelia Wells & Archie Murray
December 24, 1889 - January 15, 1967

James Harmon Wells
July 10, 1890 - February 28, 1964

Eddy Wells
1890

Paul Wells
January 15, 1895 - September 20, 1912

Lannie Wells
1899

Ella Bertha Stokes was born August 5, 1892 and she died May 13, 1981 in Duplin County, North Carolina. She is the daughter of Aronia Stokes and Curtis Hall. She married William Henry Batts January 11, 1914 in Duplin County, North Carolina. He was born January 6, 1887 and he died May 13, 1981 in Rose Hill, Duplin County, North Carolina. He is the son of Isaac and Sennie Batts. From this union eleven children are born.

Lemie Clarence Batts & Annie Gale Smith
November 4, 1914 - January 24, 1999

Rosie Lee Batts
January 28, 1916 - October 20, 2005

Cannie Roberta Batts Crumpler
October 6, 1917 - July 1992

Johnnie E. Batts
1920

Toyie Essell Batts & Vernell Hill
September 7, 1922 - February 13, 1981

Essie Virmell Batts Usher
February 12, 1924 - May 13, 1981

Wyanza & Helen Lenora Batts
1927 - April 30, 2012

Nicie R. Batts & Paul Junius Williams
1929

Louis J. Batts
1933

Daisy R. Batts & Andrew Junior Dixon
August 1933

Ella Mae Batts & Percy Junior Fennell
October 28, 1935 - November 4, 1991

James Grant Sharpless was born August 15, 1868 and he died August 1, 1960 in Cypress Creek, Duplin County, North Carolina. He is the son of John and Lucy Jane Sharpless. He married Sarah Moore. She was born August 27, 1866 and she died September 13, 1942 in Cypress Creek, Duplin County, North Carolina. She is the daughter of Louisa Moore. From this union seven children were born.

Mary Lillie Sharpless & Wiliam J. Forman
February 11, 1890 - September 24, 1977

John William Sharpless & Erie Catherine Kenan
June 10, 1892 - June 12, 1939

Oscar James Sharpless Sr. & Bertha Batts
November 4, 1895 - June 1, 1997

James Tate Sharpless & Queenie Victoria Judge
July 4, 1998 - February 19, 1959

Bertha Sharpless & Job Stallings, Ben Whitley
October 7, 1901 - February 29, 1975

Floretta Mae Sharpless & Foster Lee Blount
March 14, 1904 - January 17, 1994

Edward Sharpless & Dorotha Stokes
October 1, 1906 - February 11, 1979

Duffy Hayes Sharpless & Kay M. Blango, Alma Creola Jones
September 20, 1908 - September 17, 1983

Samuel Catillo Sharpless
Son of Oscar Grant Sharpless

Eunice Odell Sharpless Parker
daughter of James Tate Sharpless

Annie Ruth Sharpless Murray
daughter of Oscar James Sharpless

108

Andrew Wells was born in December of 1855 and no death date was found on him. He is the son of Alfred Wells and Clarissa Jacobs. He married Lucy Jane Carr December 14, 1876 in Duplin County, North Carolina. She was born July 4, 1857 and she died May 21, 1925 in Rose Hill, Duplin County, North Carolina. She is the daughter of Richard Carr and Annie J. Boney. From this union eight children were born.

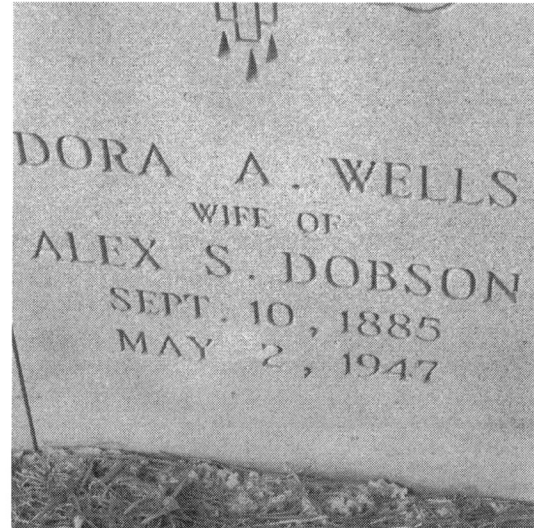

Lucy Katerine Boney Pearsall

Louberta Wells & George Kelly
1881 - September 5, 1926

Nettie Wells & Anthony Pickett
1882 - 1June 14, 1946

Bettie Wells & James Owen Newkirk
April 15, 1886 - May 20, 1957

Armelia Wells & Archie Murray
December 24, 1889 - January 15, 1967

James Harmon Wells
July 10, 1890 - February 28, 1964

Eddy Wells
1890

Paul Wells
January 15, 1895 - September 20, 1912

Lannie Wells
1899

James Dudley Monk was born November 13, 1870 and he died December 22, 1961 in Magnolia, Duplin County, North Carolina. He is the son of Dudley Monk and Luphemia A. Nixon. He married Martha Stanford. She was born February 23, 1875 and she died April 5, 1957. She is the daughter of Simon and Leah Olive Stanford.

Carrie Monk Southerland

Ed Dudley Monk

Mattie Lee Monk Williams Dobson

Carrie Mae Monk & David Southerland
August 13, 1895 - August 21, 1970

Robin Monk
1896

Edward Dudley Monk & Marie Allen
April 25, 1898 - August 19, 1999

Armittie Esther Monk & William Williams
January 24, 1900 - August 1, 2002

McKinley Monk
1903

John F. Monk
1906

Mattie Lee Monk & Theodore Rooscvelt Williams
June 22, 1909 - August 13, 1995

Etlar Louise Monk & James Washington Mainor Sr.
April 23, 1912 - October 10, 2003

Pearl Monk
1916

Geneva B. Monk
April 1, 1916 - January 1, 2011

Neal Boney Fennell was born September 3, 1894 and he died Mary 21, 1961 in Rose Hill, Duplin County, North Carolina. He is the son of Dimon and Patsy Brown Fennell. He married Lula Coston December 18, 1906 in Duplin County, North Carolina. She was born April 13, 1886 and she died September 1, 1970 in Rose Hill, Duplin County, North Carolina. She is the daughter of Miles Coston and Mittie R. Robinson. From this union nine children were born.

Mary Lilly Fennell & Walter Evans
October 16, 1907 - August 5, 2006

Bessie Louise Fennell Coston
August 26, 1909 - August 17, 1999

Joe & Eula Fennell
August 27, 1912 -

Bertis Fennell
November 17, 1914 - November 18, 1941

Susie Fennell & Richard Pollock
April 17, 1916 - July 8, 1985

James Fennell
1918 - February 2, 1939

Annie Olivia Fennell Wallace
December 2, 1923 - March 20, 1974

Willie Pearl Fennell
August 17, 1926 - November 27, 2016

Gertrude Fennell
1927

Peter Farrior was born in February of 1840 and he died September 12, 1917 in Warsaw, Duplin County, North Carolina. He married Cherry Middleton in 1866 in Duplin County, North Carolina. She was born in 1852 and no death date was found on her. From this union fifteen children were born.

Ella Farrior
1865 - November 8, 1925

Dolly A. Farrior & Joseph Herring
1867 - February 19, 1924

Sally Mary Farrior & John McArthur
1868 - August 19, 1943

Ella F. Farrior & John Mcarthur
1871 - November 8, 1925

William P. Farrior
1874

Isaac James Farrior & Neal Brown
March 20, 1875 - December 22, 1954

Priscilla Farrior & Charles Henry Kenan
September 15, 1879 - June 1, 1918

Rachel Farrior & Joseph Williams
1885 - September 22, 1930

John D. Farrior
March 25, 1885 - May 1967

Julia C. Farrior
1883 - February 16, 1949

Dock Hosea & Maggie Farrior
March 15, 1885 - June 5, 1967

Noah Farrior
February 1882

Mary M. Farrior
July 10, 1889 - January 25, 1958

Percy Farrior
February 4, 1887 - April 29, 1936

Jennie Farrior

William N. Farrior

Isaac James and Nealie Farrior

Son of Dock Hosea & Maggie Farrior

Bryant Miller was born in 1859 and he died November 9, 1930 in Kennasville, Duplin County, North Carolina. he is the son of Henry Miller. He married Jemima McIver November 15, 1878 in Duplin County, North Carolina. She was born in 1861 and no death date was found on her. From this union twelve children were born. Bryant later married Minnie Jarmon. She was born June 12, 1880 and she died April 25, 1946 in Kenansville, Duplin County, North Carolina. She is the daughter of Mathis and Fannie Jarmon. From this union eight children were born.

Malinda Miller & John Wesley McGowan
1878 - May 6, 1928

Jane Miller
1879

Lucy Miller & David Miller
1883 - January 23, 1948

Abbie Miller & Jacob Chestnut
1882 -

Lee Miller
July 15, 1885 - March 1, 1935

Arthur Miller & Mary Wallace
1889 - May 10, 1939

Sallie Miller & Willie Glaspie
1891 - September 12, 1943

Ophelia Miller & Shade Glaspie
November 27, 1889 - January 9, 1943

Douglass Miller & Lena Barden
January 2, 1890 - May 18, 1962

Noah Miller & Callie Outlaw
April 27, 1888 - December 3, 1964

Darner Miller & John Byrd
July 6, 1900 - August 21, 1972

Margie Miller & Joe Hill Smith
April 1895 - January 29, 1935

2nd Wife Minnie Jarmon children

Willis Miller
January 31, 1902

Junius Miller
1904

Arnetta Miller & James A. Miller
December 25, 1908 - November 3, 1988

Cloria Miller
March 24, 1910 - February 20, 1981

Matthew Miller & Daisy Outlaw
September 16, 1913 - June 10, 1991

Simuel Miller
1914

Minnie Frances Miller & Frank McIver
1912

Gurnie Miller
November 9, 1917 - July 11, 1988

Duplin County

African American Churches

SMITH CHAPEL BAPTIST CHURCH

Warsaw, North Carolina

Founded in 1873 by Dundy Williams, Dudley Smith, Kator Smith, Hillery Smith, Square Williams and Mattie Jarman

FIRST BAPTIST CHURCH CHARITY

Greenevers, North Carolina

Founder Rev. Council Fennell

FAISON CHAPEL CHURCH
Warsaw, North Carolina

Founded in 1889
First Pastor Rev. J. Malachi Newkirk
First Deacons

FIRST BAPTIST CHURCH
Bowden, North Carolina

Founded in 1901
Founder: Rev. J. R. Cole

FIRST BAPTIST CHURCH
Magnolia, North Carolina

Founded in 1867
Organized by Rev. Henry Lee

FIRST BAPTIST CHURCH
Chinquapin, North Carolina

Founded in 1874. The first Pastor of the church was Rev. W. C. Cowan

ADORAM BAPTIST CHURCH
Wallace, North Carolina

Founded in 1876 by Patrick Murray, Isaac C. Powers, Jacob Murphy, James McMillian

BETHOLITE BAPTIST CHURCH
Magnolia, North Carolina

Founded in 1880 Rev. Albert Minor helped to get this church established. George W. Davis, James Tate, Toomer Johnson were the first Trustees

CHRISTIAN CHAPEL BAPTIST CHURCH #1

Rose Hill, North Carolina

Founded in 1884

FIRST BAPTIST CHURCH

Rose Hill, North Carolina

Founded in 1887
Organized by: John Fussell, Ed Murphy, Bob Murphy, Eliza Jane Newkirk, Susan Newkirk, and Mittie Newkirk. First Pastor was Rev. George Davis

FIRST BAPTIST CHURCH
Teachy, North Carolina

Founded in 1896 also known as Alderman's Chapel Rev. W. H. Alderman, Robert S. Alderman, G. P. Alderman, Harriette Alderman Brown, Rev. S. P. Alderman, Deacon P.S. Alderman, James Carlton and R. T. Alderman

GRAHAM CHAPEL CHURCH
Pink Hill, North Carolina

Founded in 1921
Rev. R. V. Graham, Rev. A. H. Dixon and W. B. Sacclu organized the church

DAISY'S CHAPEL MISSIONARY BAPTIST CHURCH

Beulaville,

Daisy's Chapel was created around 1921. The names of the original trustees on the deed are: Mr. Richard Evans, Mr. Christopher Columbus Chasten, Mr. Willoughby Parker, and Mr. John Chasten. Our church is named for Mr. Christopher Chasten's daughter whose name was Daisy Chasten Dixon. She was married to one of our first deacons, Mr. Wright Dixon.

PETER'S TABERNACLE BAPTIST CHURCH

Wallace, North Carolina

Founded 1870

UNION WESLEY A.M.E. ZION CHURCH
Mount Olive, North CArolina

Founded in 1919

MT. SINAI BAPTIST CHURCH
Wallace, North Carolina

Founded in 1933
Rev. C. D Fennell was the first pastor.
First Deacon Board: Roy McGee and Miles Bryant

HINES CHAPEL FREEWILL BAPTIST CHURCH

WARSAW, NORTH CAROLINA

Founded in 1915

SALEM CHAPEL FREEWILL BAPTIST CHURCH

Pink Hill, North Carolina

Founded in 1868
Rev. Soloman Ellis, Bill Smith, Bill Miller, Alf Outlaw, Eunice Smith, Ward Smith

MT. ZION UNITED HOLY CHURCH

Warsaw, North Carolina

Founded in 1933
Founded in the home of Lizzie Frederick. Rev. Brewington was the first pastor. First deacons were Rich Williams and Leslie Cooper

PEARSALL CHAPEL UNITED HOLY CHURCH

Kenansville, North Carolina

Founded in 1930
Rev. Carl Hasty was the first pastor.

SAINT PETER UNITED HOLY CHURCH

Magnolia, North Carolina

Founded in 1901
Prayer meeting started in the home of Looney Dixon.
Emmaline Newkirk Shepard, Lizzie Williams Pigford, Mary Hussey, Maggie Bowden, Mary Beatty and Hattie Carr. First building was called Called Looney's Chapel in honor of Looney Dixon.

MIRACLE REVIVAL CHURCH

Warsaw, North Carolina

ISLAND CREEK AME CHURCH

Rose Hill, North Carolina

Founded 1886
Trustees: Dudley Dickson, Columbus Bryant, Fortune Maxwell, Samuel Boney and Criston Wells

NEW BETHEL AME CHURCH

Rose Hill, North Carolina

Founded in 1875
First Trustees: Daniel Merritt and James Bryant

ROCKFISH AME CHURCH

TEACHY, NORTH CAROLINA

Founded in 1878

ST. JAMES AME CHURCH

Keansville, North Carolina

Founded in 1870 founded by John Carlton, Charles Moore, John Brinson, Ramsey Carlton, and Ned Herring

HOLY TEMPLE HOLINESS CHURCH

Calypso, North Carolina

Founded in 1918
Rev. H. E. Parker

THE WORD CHURCH AND DELIVERANCE CENTER

Greenevers, North Carolina

Founded in September of 2009 By Pastor Larry Hooks

HALLSVILLE MISSIONARY BAPTIST CHURCH

Hallsville, North Carolina

Founded in 1867
First pastor was William H. Fennell

GUIDING STAR UNITED HOLY CHURCH

Rose Hill, North Carolina

Founded in 1923
First Pastor was Elder F. D. Rigford

MOSES CHAPEL CHRCH OF CHRIST DISCIPLE OF CHRIST
Faison, North Carolina

Founded in 1907 By Rev. Thomas McLaurin. Founding members Mattie Faison, Annie Stevens, Narcissus Lee, Clarica Whitfield, Lizie Artis, Daniel Shine, Ross Herring, L. J. Mosley, Samuel Faison

BURNING BUSH HOLY CHURCH
Faison, North Carolina

Founded in 1867 Formally known as Bear Swamp Church Thomas Parker, Ned Dixon, Bill Shaw, James Jeff Faison, Bill Faison

FIRST BAPTIST CHURCH
Calypso, North Carolina

Founded in 1914
Rev. Malachi J. Newkirk
First Deacons: C. R. Knighten, Joe C. Smith, Matthew Grantham, Lacy Robinson, Sibby Robinson, and Amos Robinson

ST. LEWIS BAPTIST CHURCH
Chinquipin, North Carolina

Founded in 1877
Sita Lewis donated the land for the church and the church was named St. Lewis in her honor. Rev. John Fennell was the founder and the first pastor.

ST. PAUL AME CHURCH
Teachy, North Carolina

Founded in 1880

ST. PETER AME CHURCH
Warsaw, North Carolina

Founded in 1888
Charter members: Holly Williams and wife Martha, Dorothy Hill, Ranson McGee, Mr and Mrs. Josh Wilson

BIG ZION AME ZION CHURCH

Kenansville, North Carolina

Founded in 1883
Commitee
G. Miller, Peter White, Bryant McIver, John Wesley McGowan, J. W. Miller
Rev. D. J. McDowell, Pastor

NEW ELDERS CHAPEL AME ZION CHURCH

Magnolia, North Carolina

Founded in 1879

ST. JAMES AME ZION CHURCH

Magnolia, North Carolina

Founded in 1878
Re. J. T. Newberry
First trustees: Amos Parker, Wiley Sellars, Thomas Morrisey, Hopton Moore, and George Boyette

ST. STEVENS AME ZION CHURCH

Warsaw, North Carolina

Founded in 1885

FIRST BAPTIST CHURCH
Kenansville, North Carolina

Founded in 1866
Founded by Thomas Parker

ST. JOHN BAPTIST CHURCH
Wallace, North Carolina

Founded in 1900 as a bible study by Abb Williams, (first organized group in 1939) with Rev. D. C. Fennell was the first pastor

NEW CHRISTIAN CHAPEL BAPTIST CHURCH

Rose Hill, North Carolina

Founded in 1943
Rev. C. R. Murray was the first pastor

FIRST MISSIONARY BAPTIST CHURCH

Warsaw, North Carolina

Founded in 1867
Formally known as Bear Swamp Church
Thomas Parker, Ned Dixon, Bill Shaw, James Jeff Faison, Bill Faison

RAINBOW BAPTIST CHURCH
Warsaw, North Carolina

Founded in 1906
By Deacon Alonza
Glaspie

THE MOUNT CHURCH
Chinquapin, North Carolina

June 14, 1974 by Elder
Carrie B. Graham

DAISY'S CHAPEL MISSIONARY BAPTIST CHURCH

Chinquapin, North Carolina

Founded in 1920
Rev. Duncan Fryar was the first pastor

FRIENDSHIP BAPTIST CHURCH

Rose Hill, North Carolina

Founded in 1874
Rev. Roash Robinson
First deacons were Briston Fussell, Diamond Fennell, Jack Williams and Dennis Crumpler

FULL GOSPEL TABERNACLE

Calypso, North Carolina

Founded in 1972 by Pastor Minnie Baker

NEW FIRST BAPTIST CHURCH

Kenansville, North Carolina

Building dedicated in February of 1990

SHAW TEMPLE AME ZION CHURCH

Rose Hill, North Carolina

SAINT LUKE UNITED HOLY CHURCH

Rosehill, North Carolina

MT. ZION COMMUNITY CHURCH

Warsaw, North Carolina

SAINT MATHEWS AME ZION CHURCH

Pink Hill, North Carolina

NEW SALEM CHAPEL FWB CHURCH

Pink Hill, North Carolina

MACEDONIA APOSTOLIC HOLINESS CHURCH

Bowden, North Carolina

PRAYER OF FAITH EVANGELISTIC CHURCH

Warsaw, North Carolina

ST. STEVENS HOLY CHURCH

Mount Olive, North Carolina

GREATER YESHUWA TEMPLE CHURCH
Wallace, North Carolina

BYRD'S CHAPEL CHURCH
Rose Hill, North Carolina

PRAYER OF FAITH EVANGELISTIC CHURCH

Warsaw, North Carolina

GREATER CORNERSTONE APOSTOLIC

Magnolia, North Carolina

HARVEST TIME FAMILY MINISTRY
Wallace, North Carolina

MOUNT PLEASANT HOLINESS CHURCH
Wallace, North Carolina

KINGDOM MINISTRIES
Calypso, North Carolina

HILLS CHAPEL BAPTIST CHURCH
Faison, North Carolina

MACEDONIA UNITED HOLY CHURCH
Beulaville, North Carolina

THE PENTECOSTAL CHURCH OF GOD
Beulaville, North Carolina

ST. MARY'S UNITED HOLY CHURCH

Kenansville, North Carolina

ST LUKE MISSIONARY BAPTIST CHURCH

Kenansville, North Carolina

DUPLIN COUNTY AFRICAN AMERICAN CEMETERIES

DUPLIN COUNTY AFRICAN AMERICAN CEMETERIES

Barnes Cemetery
Bonham Road

Bessie Mae Oliver Barnes
Carolyn Diane Barnes
James Cephus Barnes
PVT. James Thomas Barnes
James W. Barnes
Willie Thomas Barnes
Dwight Cooley
Mary Jane Coley
Hettie B. Crumpler
Thomas Elliott Crumpler
Mattie Britton Oliver
Amandy Harrison Partlow
Darlene Williams

DUPLIN COUNTY AFRICAN AMERICAN CEMETERIES

Outlaw Cemetery
Kenansville, North Carolina

Michael Sincere Cole
Derrick A. Fillyaw
Irene O. Highsmith
James O. Jarman
Daisy O. Miller
Matthew Miller
Edmond Outlaw
George F. Outlaw
Harold Lee Outlaw
Hilton Outlaw
Kelvin Laverre Outlaw
Lou A Outlaw
Norman Outlaw
Wanda O. Outlaw
Willie A. Outlaw
Willie Outlaw Jr.

DUPLIN COUNTY AFRICAN AMERICAN CEMETERIES

Smith Chapel Church Cemetery
Kenansville, North Carolina

Kattie Willean Borden
Norman Marion Borden
Ruby F. Chadwick
Donald Hall
Frank McIver Jr.
Arabelle M. Miller
Gloria Miller
Gurnice Miller
Minnie F. Miller
Preston Miller
Mildred J. Platt
Cora Williams
Delois Williams
Dundy Williams
Gene Williams
Lucille R. Williams

DUPLIN COUNTY AFRICAN AMERICAN CEMETERIES

Bryant Miller Cemetery
Kenansville, North Carolina

Bryant J. Glaspie
Edgar Glaspie Jr.
Johnnie Glaspie
Margaret M. Glaspie
Albert Miller
Bryant M. Miller
James Carnell Miller
Mamie D. Miller
Yvonne G Miller
Leroy Russell
Mary Jane Russell
Craig Smith Jr.
Rosa Glaspie Smith

DUPLIN COUNTY AFRICAN AMERICAN CEMETRIES

Dobson Cemetery
Magnolia, North Carolina

Johnny R. Dobson
Lacy J. Dobson
Lillie C. Dobson
Lott L. Dobson
General Dobson
Mable E. Dobson
Mary Dobson
Mary C. Dobson
Mary Emma Faison Dobson
Mavious Dobson
Maxie Dobson
Minnie Louis Dobson
Moses Dobson
Needham Dobson
Octavious Dobson
Paul E. Dobson
Sarah B. Dobson
Stacy A. Dobson
Sudie Farrior Dobson
Nathaniel Dobson

Mattie Leah Williams Dobson
Raymond Dobson
William A. Dobson
William Dobson
Maddie B. Dobson Green
Bernice Kea
Mary Bell Sloan Kea
Wanda Kea
Katie Fields
Preston Leggett Jr.
James E. McArthur
Ludell B. McArthur
James McKiver
Jannette Mathis
John H. Moore
John R. Moore
Joseph Moore
Kelvin L. Moore

Bertha Murphy
David Robinson Jr.
Sarah Dobson Robison
Joseph A. Tyler
James Thorb
Vera Dobson Williams
Fernando Guy Whitehead
Ophelia D. Moore Whitehead
Susie R. Zanders

DUPLIN COUNTY AFRICAN AMERICAN CEMETRIES

Cleo Miller Cemetery
Airport Road - Kenansville, North Carolina

Anthony McKiver
Cleo Miller
Howard Miller
Isiah Miller
Dossie Taylor
Paulette T. Torrey

DUPLIN COUNTY AFRICAN AMERICAN CEMETERIES

Alderman Cemetery
Wallace, North Carolina

Annie L. Alderman
Annie M. Alderman
Ben Alderman Jr.
Benjamin Alderman Sr.
Derry Frank Alderman
Helen Murphy Alderman
Lula Mae Alderman
Rachel Ann Graham Alderman
Robert Sherman Alderman
Robert T. Alderman
Rev. William Henry Alderman
Annie Power Atkinson
Rev. Golia Atkinson
Robert E. Baysden
Melissa L. Boney
Liston Boykin Jr.
Obbie L. Boykins
Annie M. Brown
Hattie Alderman Brown
Evelyn C. Bryant
Walter Bryant Jr.

Arthur Bernice Carlton Sr.
Fisher C. Alderman Carlton
James Carlton
James Carlton
James Gregory Carlton
Mary Bert McMillan Carlton
Rebecca Highsmith Carlton
Seymour P. Carlton
Raphael Waymon Carlton
Willie Banks Carlton
Annie R. Coston
J. Herman Coston
Lilie H. Curry
Henry H. Curry
Henry Davis
Gloria C. Dixon
Professor Carl Winfred Dobbins
Hattie Carlton Dobbins
Duney Dudley
Dorothy Sutton Ellis

Patsy William Flowers
Enda Fryer
Henry Martel Fryer
Bertha L. hayes
Willie Hayes
Elouise S. Herring
Bettie Highsmith
Herman Highsmith
Sylvia Highsmith
William E. Highsmith
Annie Wells Howard
Theodore C. Howard
Robert Keith
Bruce Lipscomb Jr.
Bruce Lipscomb
Marie Boney Lipscomb
Pearl W. Mathis
William E. Mathis
Hellena Lane McKinnon
Roosevelt McKinnon
Sam McKinnon
Johnnie Milton
Johnnie Milton Jr.

DUPLIN COUNTY AFRICAN AMERICAN CEMETERIES

Alderman Cemetery
Wallace, North Carolina

James R. Moore
Walter Murphy
Gerald Murray Jr.
Gerald D. Murray
Lena Boney Murray
Leatha A. Murrell
Mary F. Newkirk
Sarah Corbett Newkirk
Allen McKinley Peterson
Armous Peterson
Edith M. Peterson
Elijah Peterson
Ethel Alderman Peterson
Robert C. Peterson
Sarah S. Peterson
Willie C. Petterson
James allen Smith Jr.
James T. Smith
James W. Smith
Lattice P. Smith
Lucille Davis Smith

Mary Alice Alderman Spearman
Ellis Sutton
Louisa Newkirk Sutton
Mary N. Sutton
Edith M. Taylor
Herman L. Teachey
Ida G. Teachey
Julis Teachy
F. C. Thompson
Lillie Bell Hufham Thompson
Charlie Wells Jr.
Charlie Wells Sr.
Estella Holmes Wells
Hattie M. Wells
James Ollen Wells
Ricole Renee Wells
Roger Louis Wells
Timothy Wells
Beatrice S. Williams
Jim C. Williams
Ronald B. Williams

DUPLIN COUNTY AFRICAN AMERICAN CEMETERIES

Big Zion AME Zion Church Cemetery
Kenansville, North Carolina

Esther Mae Miller Buckram
Trevor Buckram
Charlene Brooks Faison
Alice Hazel Herring
Gracie Ann Chamber Herring
Irene Jones
Melvin Bobby Jones
Alex McIver
Denise Maria McIver
Elmiree McIver
Johnie M. McIver

William J. McIver
Annie E. Miller
Clemith E. Miller
David Miller Jr.
David O. Miller
Doretha Miller
Edna Mae Miller
Esther Mae Miller
Gregory N. Miller
Henry Albert Miller
Jerry L. Miller

Jimmie G. Miller
Jonathan Miller
Leo Miller
Mary E. Miller
Mertie Miller
Richard Miller
Samuel W. Miller
Sudie Miller
Thomas Miller
Herman L. outlaw
Mimie E. Pearsal

DUPLIN COUNTY AFRICAN AMERICAN CEMETERIES

McGowan Family Cemetery
Kenansville, North Carolina

Rufus Ashford
Dacia Yvette Bass
Annie McGee Boney
Martha Ann Bradshaw
Juanita Miller Broadie
Lucy Ann Bryant
Liza M. Carlton
Willard Carlton Sr.
Leroy Dixon
Melinda Dixon
Lucy M. Garner
Lucy Jarmon
Henrietta Jarmon
James Randolph
Andrew Floyd McGee
Artis Lee McGee
Beatrice McGee
Bernice McGee
James McGee
Sula McGee
John McGee

William E. McGee
Emma Ruth McGee
George McGowan
Henry Clay McGowan
Henrietta McGowan
Henry McGowan
Henry Ned McGowan
John W. McGowan
John W. McGowan
Johnny Lee McGowan
Lucille O. McGowan
Lucy McGowan
Margie M. McGowan
Martha M. McGowan
Mary McGowan
Nathan McGowan
Percy E. McGowan
Rosa Mitchell McGowan
Shirley M. McGowan

Bryan McIver
Louiser McIver
William McIver
Amanda J. Miller
Carolyn Miller
Clayborn Miller
Gladys M. Miller
Hattie E. Miller
John William Miller
Jack Miller
Joseph C. Miller
Mary A. Miller
Phillip C. Miller
Sudie Miller
William Thomas Miller
Cornelia McGowan Outlaw
Solomon Outlaw
Mattie M. Rochelle
Elouise Savage
Alberta M. Shumbert
Nathan Roy Smith
Millie Wallace

DUPLIN COUNTY AFRICAN AMERICAN AMERICAN CEMETERIES

Boone Family Cemetery
Rosehill, North Carolina

Alice Howard Boone
Doctor D. Boone
Exloner Greene Fowler Boone
Henry C. Boone
Henry King Boone
James F. Boone
Janie Merriett Boone
Jitter Lloyd Boone Sr.
Larry Davis Boone
Lloyd Thomas Boone
Mary E. Williams Boone
Molcey Mathis Boone
Nancy Louise Mathis Boone
Robert James Boone
Sophia Doretha Boone
William Tyrone Boone
Willie George Boone
Jim Henry Bridges Jr.
Robert Edward Bridges
Sylvia Boone Bridges
Bertha Lee Chestnutt Bryant
George Frank Carlton
Jasper Z. Carlton
Katie E. Carlton
Quortez D. J. Carlton
Fitchure Alonzo Chestnut
PFC Franklin H. Chestnut
Bertha M. Cobb
Leon O. Collins Jr.
Ada Gillespie Frederick
King David Frederick
Bertha M. Graham
Kenneth H. Graham
William Graham Jr.
William Graham Sr.
Charlie J. Hardy
Sarah Boone Hardy
Smithia Boone Hardy
Walter Hardy
Willie Frank Hardy
Canary J. Hooks
Kenneth C. Hooks
Mary Lillie Wells Hooks
Matthews Hooks Jr.
PFC Matthew Hooks III
Smithley Cleo Jones
M. M.
William E. Newkirk
Alonzo Raines
Eva Marie Locklear Raines
Mabel C. Raines
Eva B. Rhodes
Dudley D. Rolle
Edna Mildred Newkirk Rolle
Bertha B. Tony
Anna Belle Frederick Wilson
Mary Louise Wilson

DUPLIN COUNTY AFRICAN AMERICAN AMERICAN CEMETERIES

Hall Family Cemetery
Waycross - Magnolia, North Carolina

Nancy Boss
John Bryant
Rosie Bryant
Baby Boy Dixon
Mattie A. Dixon
Minnie Hall Dixon
Minnie Henry Dixon
Blanche Hall
Caroline Hall
Charliee Hall
Charlie Henry Hall
Eddie Graham Hall
Ella Hall
Hannah Jane Hall
Harriet J. Hall
James M. Hall

John Henry Hall
Joseph Hall
Judah Hall
M. Dennie Hall
Mittie Parris Hall
Walter R. Hall
Chancey Herring
Hattie M. Herring
John Herring
Franklin Isaiah Huffman
Eddie G. Merritt
Jonathan Merritt
Neicy E. Merritt
Rev. R.C. Merritt
Susan Anner Merritt
W. Sidberry Southerland

Eaenest Bank Williams
John James Williams
Layafette Williams
Mary Wiliams

DUPLIN COUNTY AFRICAN AMERICAN AMERICAN CEMETERIES

St. Lewis Cemetery
Chinquapin, North Carolina

Maidie Judge Adams
Annie G. Batts
Ella Betha Hall Batts
Emmalina Batts
L Clarence Batts
Susanna Kenan Batts
Pvt. Zollie Batts
Fannie Whitley Batts Farrior
Emily Williams Berry
Mary Blanchard
David James Brown
Grover L. Brown
Mamie Rochelle Brown
Kinnie Bertha Pickett Crawly
Alonzo Croombs
Mary S. Croombs
Geraldine B. Crooms
Cunnie R. Crumpler
Retha B. Donaldson
Calvin Evans
Beulah McFarland
George H. Farland
joseph R. Farland
Lorna Farland

Nettie E. Farland
Ruth Ann Farland
James W. Graham
Leon Graham Sr.
Victoria Lee Whitley Graham
Eddie Gray Hall
George M. Hill
George Robert Hill
James E. Hill
Ora Usher Lee Hill
Stacy Hill
Sula K. Hill
Candies G. Humphrey
Maggie S. James
Alexander Judge
Alexander Judge Sr.
David Owen Judge
Dudley Gleamon Judge
Fannie Lee Pickett Judge
George Earnest Judge
James Henry Judge

Jane E. Judge
Linston Judge
Loney D. Judge
Louis Judge
Margaret Murray Judge
Mariah Judge
Mary Cassie Judge
Moses Judge
Alonza Kelly
Monroe Kelly
Sylvia Kenan Kelly
Charles Wright Kenan
Franklin Montgomery Kenan
Horace H. Kenan
Julia A Williams Kenan
Montgomery Kean
Virginia Dare Hall Kenan
Mary E. Lanier
Edmond Warren G. Harding Lee
Henry Fitzhugh Lee
Henry I. Lee
Vina Catherine Murray Lee
Carrie F. Moore
Wanda Gail Moore

163

DUPLIN COUNTY AFRICAN AMERICAN AMERICAN CEMETERIES

St. Lewis Cemetery
Chinquapin, North Carolina

Glen Dale Morris
Elizabeth P. Moses
Goley T. Murphy
Newberry Murray
Alfred E. Pickett
Anthony Hill Pickett Jr.
Cecil James Pickett
Connie Pickett
Dundy Pickett
Easter W. Pickett
Eliza Jane Lee Pickett
Elizabeth Pickett
Eric L. Pickett
Eula J. Pickett
George Pickett
Hilton Pickett
James E. Pickett
James Roscoe Pickett
Joe H. Pickett
Lionel Pickett
Lonnie E. Pickett
Louise S. Pickett
Lonnie E. Pickett

Louise S. Pickett
Louvena Pickett
Marlon Pickett
Mary Bella Judge Pickett
Norma S. Pickett
Norwood Pickett
Preston Elijah Pickett
Rossie Pickett Jr.
Terrence D. Pickett
Vincent C. Pickett
Willie A. Pickett
Willie A. Pickett Jr.
Willia A Pickett Sr.
Willie C. Pickett
Willie Rouse Pickett
Nicey B. Pope
Ronald Lee Sharpless
Kent M. Smith
Cherly Southerland
Bessie K. Stokes

Enda P. Thomas
Annie T. Tyler
Damen M. Tyler
Essie B. Usher
Johnnie Lee Usher
Martha B. Waters
Atha Jane Batts Whitley
Robert Pen Whitley
Alvin Williams
Bessie P. William s
Cicero Williams
Dennis Williams
Fletcher Williams
James Tate Williams
Jethro William Sr.
Leroy Williams
Mae Dell Williams
Maggie R. Williams
Nellie M. Williams
Paul Williams Jr.
Phil A. Williams
Winford Williams
Evaline Edna Williams

DUPLIN COUNTY AFRICAN AMERICAN AMERICAN CEMETERIES

Middleton Cemetery
Kenansville, North Carolina

Charlotte F. Adams
James Nathaniel Adams
Natalie Faye Adams
Dawson Andrews
Lucy Ashford
Perry Ashford
Hattie Louise Austin
Richard Bass Jr.
Rev. Edward Lee Batts
Teritha Hill Batts
Daisy M. Bell
Benjamin Belle
Isham Belle Jr.
Isham Leonard Belle Sr.
Sallie Elizabeth Belle
Irvin Edward Belton
Willie Benson
Daisy J. Best
Alberta Bracey
James A. Bradshaw
Natalene Bradshaw
Charles Brandon II
Dorothy J. Brandon
Davis Lloyd Brinson
David T. Brinson
Emily W. Brinson
Katie L. Brinson
Annie L. Brown
Jonathan Brown
Mattie M. Brown
Preston D. Brown
Thomas Brown
Virginia Bell Brown
Hattie B. Bubkette
Darner Miller Byrd
John Henry Byrd
Burnice Carlton
Lacy Carlton Jr.
Moses McIver Carlton
William Joseph Carlton
William Joseph Carney
Dilsia F. Carr
Leeourtha G. Carr
Patricia Ann Freeman Carr
Tyson Carr
Lee P. Chrome
Sequan Banks Coe
Fannie Mae Ellis Cooper
John Wesley Cooper
Luara Washington Cooper
Marie Murray Cooper
Marie M. Cooper
Mattie Catherine Cooper
Moses Cooper II
Moses Cooper Jr.
Hattie Cotton
Laura Davis
Stanley DeAnre Dawson
James D. Dixon
Lynn S. Dixon
Nathaniel Dixon Sr.
Daniel Hill Dobson
David Dobson
Helen R. Dobson
Lillie Mae Dobson
Jhonson Estime
Burnice Faison
Cora Lee Kenan Faison
Dorothy Mae Outlaw Faison
Ellis Faison

DUPLIN COUNTY AFRICAN AMERICAN AMERICAN CEMETERIES

Middleton Cemetery
Kenansville, North Carolina

Fred Faison Jr.
Gail Jeanette Faison
Jessie Lee Faison
Johnnie Lee Faison
Levi Faison
Robert Faison
Sarah Faison
Theodore Roosevelt Faison
Vera G. McGowan Faison
Wilhemania M. Faison
Willie Faison
Dewitt Faison
Eddie Farrior
Gertrude J. Farrior
Henry F. Farrior
Herber Farrior
Johnnie Hill Farrior
Lib Farrior
Maggie L. Farrior
Martha M. Farrior
Nellie McKiver Farrior
Reatha Mae Farrior
Rebecca Farrior
Ruth M. Farrior

Sudie S. Farrior
Tiesha N. Farrior
Tommie Farrior Jr.
William A. Farrior
William Henry Farrior
William W. Farrior
Willie A. Farrior
Joleski Kwame Floyd
Edgar Eli Frazelle
Alma Jeniata Frederick
Harold Frederick
Libbie Kenan Frederick
Luke Frederick Jr.
Baby Girl Frederick
Shade Gillespie
James W. Glasper
David E. Glaspie
Eva Glaspie
Carroll Graham
Clifton M. Graham
Eloise Graham

Ethel L. Graham
John E. Graham
John Wesley Graham
Martha Graham
Nomus L. Graham
Romus Lee Graham
Shirley Mae Graham
Williams Graham
Minisha Quita Gray
Charlie Frank Hardy
inez Henderson
Billie Marvin hill Sr.
Julius Hill
Lena Glaspie Hill
Herbert Hodges
Sarah Hodges
Sarah Jackson
Ambrose James
Barbara Wallace James
General Lee James Jr.
Katie Mae Middleton James
Annie Jones
Ben J. James
David L. jones
Eula Jones

DUPLIN COUNTY AFRICAN AMERICAN AMERICAN CEMETERIES

Middleton Cemetery
Kenansville, North Carolina

Fannie M. Jones
Julia Lee Carlton Jones
Lacy Jones
Mary Magdalene Jones
Nathaniel Jones
Pennie F. Jones
Robert E. Jones
Rosie L. Jones
Thomas Jones
Walter L. Jones
William M. Jones
Allen Terrell Jordan
Lila Gray Pearsall Judge
Elma M. Kea
Clara Lillian Southerland Kenan
Hannah Southerland Kenan
Johnie Kenan
Alex Kornegay
Martha E. Kornegay
Lila B. Latimer
Kenneth Lee Lewis
Elnora H. Manley
Mary Alice Middleton Mathis
Valeria G. Mathews

Charlie H. McArthur
Larry Donnell McArthur
Louise F. McArthur
Lucy McArthur
Gertha McGowan
Katie McIver McGowan
LouiseMcGowan
Melvia McGowan
Sylvester McGowan
Tom McGowan
Addie D. McIver
Carl McIver
Hall McIver
Rebecca Elizabeth McIver
Martha A. McIver
Allen Middleton
Annie C. Middleton
Bessie B. Middleton
Catherine Byrd Middleton
David Middleton
Donson Moore Middleton

Eugene Middleton
Herman Middleton
James J. Middleton
Jimmie E. Middleton
Jimmie Wayne Middleton
Judson Middleton
Mary Williams Middleton
Mary Belle Southerland Middleton
Richard E. Middleton
Robert G. Middleton
Robert Joe Middleton
Sallie E. Pearsall Middleton
Timothy Middleton
William E. Middleton
Albert D. Miller
Annie M. Miller
Annie Mae Miller
Cora Miller
David J. Miller
Davis Miller
Douglass Miller
Glendora Miller
Glenn Miller
Ida B. Miller
Janie Miller

DUPLIN COUNTY AFRICAN AMERICAN AMERICAN CEMETERIES

Middleton Cemetery
Kenansville, North Carolina

Jim Henry Miller
Joyce F. Miller
Leanna Miller
Leroy B. Miller
Lillie Mae Faison Miller
Mary Emma Miller
Noah Miller
Nora Leona Smith Miller
Pamela thea Brunson Miller
Perry Miller
Randolph Miller
Richard Miller
Robert E. Miller
Stephen Miller
Avis P. Moore
Beatrice I. Moore
Bryant Moore
Cora C. Moore
Henry L. Moore
Hugh F. Moore Jr.
Levi Moore
Lizzie S. Moore
Marion K. Moore
Mary Moore
Mary Lou Pearsal Moore

Matt L. Moore
Neicy Graham Moore
Wilbert Moore
Gregory Terrill Morrisey
Matt L. Moore
Neicy Graham Moore
Wilbert Moore
Gregory Terrill Morrisey
William Earl Morrisey
Deborah Ann Murray
Hester Graham Murray
Nikkio Jamal Murray
Brenda D. Newton
Fred D. Newton
Mathel J. Newton
Sarah M. Newton
Floy Dell Oglesby
James Herman Outlaw
Willie Outlaw Jr.
Arthur William Pearsall
Charlie Bland Pearsall

Chelcy Pearsall
Estella Chamber Pearsall
Leonar Pearsall
Louise Jones Pearsall
Norwwod Pearsall Jr.
Phurman Pearsall Jr.
Rosetta Elizabeth Cooper Pearsall
Steven Gary Pearsall
Charlie West Phillips
Rufus Pickett
Phyliss Fay Powell
Elouise Reeves
James Rice
Mittie E. Rice
Della M. Royal
Joseph H. Royal
Ernestine Shuler
Hannah B. Sims
Lafayette Sims
Ohie Sims
Anna Frances Miller Smith
Eddie Lee Smith
Peggy Jewel Smith
Emma R. Carlton Southerland
Hallie E. Southerland

DUPLIN COUNTY AFRICAN AMERICAN AMERICAN CEMETERIES

Middleton Cemetery
Kenansville, North Carolina

James F. Southerland Jr.
Joe Southerland
John Albert Southerland
Lillie F. Southerland
Odell C. Southerland
Susan Southerland
Daisy Stackhouse
Samuel Stackhouse
Anrico Danelle Stevenson
Tyronda A. Monroe Stevenson
Cleo M. Stewart
Susan Swinson
Lettia A. Taylor
James Durwood Tyler
Jake Washington
Shirley Rainey Washington

Martha E. White
Nathaniel White
Patrick Maurice Whitehead
Rev. Ruthel Carrol Whitehead
Alonzo Williams
Dorothy T. Williams
James Williams
Mary E. Williams
Mary Elizabeth Williams
Nina E. Williams
Peggy Lee Wilson

DUPLIN COUNTY AFRICAN AMERICAN AMERICAN CEMETERIES

Carlton-Johnson Cemetery
Kenansville, North Carolina

Robert L. Avent
johnny Barnes Jr.
Maric Barnes
Henry Boney
Cassie M. Bracey
Albert McCoy Carlton
Della Carlton
James C. Carlton
Carrie Mae Bertha Frederick Carroll
Jessie Carroll
L. Tyrone Carroll
Thelma Lois Carroll
Willie James Carrolls Jr.
Addie W. Cooper
Gladys Sutton Cooper
Lacy James Cooper
Valeria F. Cooper
Michael D. Darden
Willie Ricky Faison Jr.
Bryant James Farrior
Serethal Leanna Green Farrior
Chester Leonza Frederick Sr.
Elizabeth Brown Frederick
Elouise Register Frederick

Henry Lloyd Frederick
Henry T. Frederick
James E. Frederick
James E. Frederick
laFayette Fullwood Frederick
Leslie David Frederick
Mable B. Frederick
Margana Gillispie Frederick
Mildred Irene Frederick
Sherman Ezra Frederick
William Sherman Frederick Sr.
Willie Lee Frederick
Jannie S. Green
Minnie L. Green
Robert E. Green
William E. Green
Ida Murrill Hill
Delfinia Hodges
Harold Stanley Hodges
James A. Hodges
James Winston Hodges

Luberta Hodges
Michael thomas Hodges
Paris Hodges
Sarah Hodges
Thomas Hodges
Thomas Henry Hodges Jr.
Willie Lee Hodges
Lena M. James
Allie D. Johnson
Jessie W. Johnson
Mary Johnson
Viola Johnson
Leslie Jones
Linda Adriene McKiver Jones
Sallie Johnson Jones
Esther F. McIver
Joseph McIver
James Middleton
James Norman Middleton
Jannie Bell Middleton
Thay Monk
Mary Moore
Matthew Moore
Otis Moore

DUPLIN COUNTY AFRICAN AMERICAN AMERICAN CEMETERIES

Carlton-Johnson Cemetery
Kenansville, North Carolina

Richard Moore
Maudia P. Moss
Janice Carroll obey
Melanie Rhodes
William B. Rhodes
Esther C. Johnson Scott
Willie Mae Scott
Margaret G. Sidberry
E. Ernestine Sullivan

Alese Wallace
Willie M. Wallace
Rachel J. Weston
Larry Frank Williams
Lenora Williams
Mary F. Williams
Shade G. Williams
William J. Williams
Harry L. Wilson

DUPLIN COUNTY AFRICAN AMERICAN AMERICAN CEMETERIES

Bowden Family Cemetery
Magnolia, North Carolina

Deacon Harrison Benjamin Best Jr.
Felecia Bowden Blue
Andrew Jarron Bowden
Cicero Bowden
Geraldine Bowden
Gladys Cooper Bowden
Gladys Carr Bowden
Gloria Mae Williams Bowden
Hannah F. Bowden
James Mathis Bowden
Rivers Bowden
Ron Bowden
Thomas Allen Bowden
Vernold Bowden
Willie Bowden
Annie Pearl Daniels
James Vernon Eakins
Jessie Graham
Lou Emma Henderson
Roy Pearsall Jr.
Amie Whitehead
Mary Williams

DUPLIN COUNTY AFRICAN AMERICAN AMERICAN CEMETERIES

Moore Family Cemetery
Warsaw, North Carolina

Owen Barden
Ray Anthony Battle
Thomas Brount Beasley
PFC Thomas Dewitt Jr.
Angeiener Moore Fields
Annie M. Geigher
Allie Pearl Wilson Glaspie
Doshie Phine Graham Glaspie
John Glaspie
John Edd Glaspie
Marvin Wesley Glaspie
George Kilpatrick Jr.
Lucille Elizabeth Moore Mansell
Arette Midleton
Frank Middleton
Illya Nikolia Middleton
Mary Madgeline Middleton
Bernice Moore
Beulah Adella Carlton Moore
Causie Anna Taylor Moore
Chelcy Moore
David Moore
David Leonard Moore
Euray Preston Moore Jr.
Euray Preston Moore Sr.
Geneva Wright Moore
Isaiah Moore
Ivory Thomas Moore
James R. Moore
James Richmond Moore Jr.
James Richard Moore Sr.
Johny Shelton Moore
Katie Mae Gillespie Moore
Lawrence Dean Moore Jr.
Lawrence Dean Moore Sr.
PFC Leonard Thomas Moore
Mary Lee Moore
Mary Lou Moore
Richard Allen Moore
Ruth Mae Murphy Moore
Tenner Moore Moore
Victor Irving Moore
Wesley Moore
Willie Edward Moore
Edmund Tyron Newkirk
Johnny Darnell Philyaw
Jessie Rowe
Martha Rowe
George Vann Jr.
Andrew Wallace
Katie Moore White
Davante Tyreek Williams
Eunice Moore Williams
Jerry Lewis Williams
Argie Lee Moore Wilson
Cleveland Wilson
SSGT Elroy Wilson
SSGT James Journey Wilson

DUPLIN COUNTY AFRICAN AMERICAN AMERICAN CEMETERIES

Boney Cemetery
Greenevers, Magnolia, North Carolina

Dorothy M. Alderman
Vonder David Alderman
Shirley Hall barden
Isaac Lamar Batts
Angela Lee Boney
Bertha Mae Carr Boney
Cheryl Debise Boney
Dancie Rosevelt Boney
Ella Hill Boney
Ephraim Boney
Esther Houston Boney
Hattie Lee Boney
Rev. Holland Boney
James L. Boney
James Sprunt Boney Jr.
James Unfort Boney
Jean Pickett Boney
John Boney
John Thomas Boney
Julia Ann Pearsall Boney
Kermit Boney
Loura C. Boney
Maggie B. Boney
Mamie Gavin Boney
Mary T. Stevens Boney
Nellie Wells Boney
Oscar E. Boney
Robert Leslie Boney
Robert Leslie Boney Sr.
Robert Louis Boney
Russell Louis Boney
Russell Vernando Boney
Susan Ann McGee Boney
Walter James Boney Sr.
Willie Boney Jr.
Willie Boney Jr.
Willie Moses Boney
Barbara B. Brown
Clara Mae Boney Carr
Matilda Carr
Gary Carroll III
Minnie E. Carroll
Shelia Brown Carroll
AbigailBoney Chasten
James B. Chasten
Rovenia G. Chasten
Alfred Coston
Annie Ruth Coston
Margaret A. Dobson
Laura Lee Boney Dunn
Laura Fryar
Thelma Lee Furlow
Betsy Anna Graham
Cleveland Graham
David Graham
Nancy F. Graham
Richard Allen Graham
Sallie Graham
Sarah Boney Graham
Woodrow Graham
Edward Lamb
Frankie Loftin Lamb
Mary Marie Lamb
John S. Lanier
J. Ervin Dixon Lofton
Grover McCullough
Joseph McCullough
Lilar L. McCullough
Mathis Merritt
Bernice Carr Newkirk
Annie Boney Powers
William Joseph Powers Sr.
Lessie Mae Savage
George Esaw Staten
George T. Staten
Lossie B. Boney Wells
Walter Raleigh Wells
Glennie Whitfield
Mamie W. Williams
Willie W. Williams

DUPLIN COUNTY AFRICAN AMERICAN AMERICAN CEMETERIES

New Christian Chapel Church Cemetery
Greenevers, Magnolia, North Carolina

Edward Allen
Estella Hargrove Allen
Charlie Anthony
Wilma Mae Brown Applewhite
Arthur E. Batts
Betsy Pearl Batts
Birl Batts
Carrie T. Batts
Crettie Mae Teachey Batts
Dennis Batts
Felicea Fountaine Batts
Issac Batts Jr.
Maggie F. Batts
Mary S. Batts
Ralph Batts Raymond L, Batts
William D. Batts
Sharon Alfreda Batts Smith
Beverly J. Miller Boney
Brigette M. Boney
Charlie J. Boney Sr.
Charlie J. Boney Jr.
Clifton Boney
Douglas H. Boney
Elias Boney
George Daniel Boney
Harry Linwood Boney
Inez Boney
Isaac Vance Boney
Isabella Sarah Chasten Boney
Jim Boney
Johnnie L. Boney
Leroy Boney
Mamie A. Boney
Marshall Boney
Nancy Mae Carr Boney
Prettie L. Brown Boney
Sallie Marie Jones boney
Vassie Mae Boney
Wanda A. Boney
Willie Macy Boney
Lillie B. Brandon
Reginald L. Bridgers
Bobby Brinson
Jimmy W. Brinson
Marinda Boney Brinson
Raymond Brinson
Raymond J. Brinson
Roy Brinson
Roy Rogers Brinson
William A. Brinson
Alex Brown
Claudie Harrison Brown
Cora Brown
Essie Lene Hill Brown
Helen P. Brown
James C. Brown
James M. Brown
Johnny Ward Brown
Malton Ward Brown
Marie Brown
Myrtie J. Brown
Robert C. Brown
Robert S. Brown
Robert Solon Brown
Rudolph Brown
Rudolph Brown Jr.
Sarah B. Brown
Antron J. Canady
Beulah J. Capps
Bob Jefferson Carr
Dewitt Carr
Elbert Carr
Gaynelle C. Carr

DUPLIN COUNTY AFRICAN AMERICAN AMERICAN CEMETERIES

New Christian Chapel Church Cemetery
Greenevers, Magnolia, North Carolina

Harry Lee Carr
James C. Carr
Janie M. Carr
Katie Florence Murray Carr
Larry Allen Carr
Mary Edna Carr
Mary Martha Carr
Matthew O. Carr
Nancy Mae Batts Carr
Rev. Robert Leslie Carr
Ruthie Mae Carr
Trevor O. Carr
Wilbert James Carr
Willie R. Carr
Bessie Ann Teachy Carroll
Carrie B. Carroll
Frances Carroll
James A. Carroll
Joyce Caroll
Garlie Washburn Chasten Jr.
Reynell Angela Chasten
Della Mae Cooper
Dorothy Mae Cooper
Linzy C. Cooper

Robert E. Cooper
Vickie Lynn Cooper
Wilbert O. Cooper
James Robert Coston
Kenneth R. Coston
Gertrude Days
Addie Mae Brinson Dixon
Florence D. Dixon
Herman Lee Dixon
Hezekiah K. Dixon
Hubert Dixon
Mamie B. Dixon
Thomas J. Dixon
Thomas T. Dixon
Wilbert Dixon Jr.
James Robert Dobson
Herman R. Duckett
Lula M. Duckett
Carl E. Dunn
Clara Mae Dunn
Virginia E. Dunn

Larry Donnell Faison
Annie Doris Kenan Farlow
Andra Rena Farrior
Arthur James Farrior
Bertah C. Farrior
Charlie W. farrior
Claudie O. Farrior
Georgia B. Farrior
Jerry D. Farrior
Laddie Cokee Murray Farrior
Lottie M. Farrior
Mildred L. Farrior
Raeford Farrior Farrior
Robert P. Farrior
Sarah Newkirk Farrior
William N. Farrior
Joseph L. Fennell
Cynthia Pearsell Ferguson
Elizabeth K. Furlow
Sulla B. Gallaway
Sybil B. Goins
Alice Faye Farrior Graham
James Adrian Graham

DUPLIN COUNTY AFRICAN AMERICAN AMERICAN CEMETERIES

New Christian Chapel Church Cemetery
Greenevers, Magnolia, North Carolina

Pennie C. Matthews Graham
Queenie M. Graham
Shelton Dean Graham
Calvin Gurbeam
Billie Gray hall
Billy J. Hall
Carl Dean Hall
Bessie Gertrude Carr Hargrove
Earl Thomas Hargrove Sr.
John Hargrove
Ronnie Chester Hargrove
Willie Thad Hargrove
Wingford Page Hargrove
Daniel James Harper
James H. Hatchel
Hazel Bezell Carr Herring
Isaac Junior Herring
James Franklin Herring
Lattie V. Herring
Philander Herring
William Henry Herring
Clara H. Hobbs
Greta C. Howard
Lucy Cooper Jackson
Calvert Jamaro Jarman
Wilma H. Jarman
Willie James Johnson
Emanuel W. Jones
Henry Jones
Merlyn F. Jones
Callie Cooper Kelly
Ruth B. Kelly
Cleveland R. Kenan
Daniel H. Kenan
James Kenan
James William Kenan
John R. Kenan
Martha Tammy McCallop Kenan
Garg D. Jarmam
Iree M. Jarman
James C. Jarman
Myrtle W. Jarman
Reginald Hall Jarman
Rhonda Jarman
Sarah Elizabeth Boney Jarman
Sarah Catherine Herring McGowan
Sheron C. Mleod
Joe Nathan McMillian
Florence E. McMillian
Sarah Batts Kenan
William Kenan
Walter A. Kenion
Sarah C. Brown koonce
Sarah S. Koonce
Judy G. Langston
Mary Melissa Outlaw Lawson
Anthony McCoy Lee
Alma Brinson Loftin
Ammie O Matthews
Exie Mae Matthews
Hattie P. Matthews

DUPLIN COUNTY AFRICAN AMERICAN AMERICAN CEMETERIES

New Christian Chapel Church Cemetery
Greenevers, Magnolia, North Carolina

Iola J. Matthews
John Edmond Matthews
Jonathan Matthews
Mertie B. Matthews
Barbara Ann McCallop
William McDonald
Agnes E. McGee
Sarah J. Murphy
Ada Carr Murray
Christopher Columbus Murray
Emily Hopeshella Murray
James Murray
Lummie M. Murray
Nathen Coe Murray
Vernell Boney Murray
James Vitrus Murray
Ella K. Kenan Newkirk
Annie M. Pearsall
Norma Teachey Pearsall
Sadie Pearsall

Ea Jane Boney Pickett
Willie Mae Pickett
Mary E. Powell
Stephanie Brinson Rainy
Queen Isabell Thacker Reese
Thelma L. Reid
Betty Lou Rogers
Ethyl Lee Wallace Sanders
Esther Langston Savage
Staten Savage
Flossie D. Seally
Ruby W. Simmons
Ethel S. Sinclair
Annie M. Thompson Smith
Adell S. Cooper Stallings
Charles George Stallings
Eric Wadell Stallings
James Stallings
James Philemon Stallings

Robert Ray Stallings
Dorothy Mae Teachey
Fannie Isabelle Pearsall Teachy
Sandy Mack Teachy
Elmer B. Thompson
Saundra Lee Pearsal Troxler
Brian A. Wade Sr.
Elizabeth Nicole Wade
Gwendolyn B. West
Janie Viola Whitehead
Judson Whitehead
Orphia C. Whitehead
Bertha J. Williams
Dwight Williams
Sadie Bell Murray Williams
Rev. Willie J. Williams
Alphonzo Ziegfield Zanders Jr.

DUPLIN COUNTY AFRICAN AMERICAN AMERICAN CEMETERIES

Adoram Baptist Church Cemetery
Wallace, North Carolina

Lillie M. Alderman
Mary Alderman
Curtis Anthony
Ella M. Anthony
Florence T. Baker
Sidney Baker
Mary F. Bannerman
Hattie Bass
Henry Bass
William C. Bass
William P. Bass
Hattie Beasley
Samuel Beasley
Lizzie Bennerman
Eugene Bennett
Mary Ann Teachey Bennett
Nora P. Bennett
Alena Blackman
Alice Beatrice Boney
Dorothy W. Boney
Ethel P. Boney
Hattie McIntyre Boney
Mary Horrell Boney
Vivian Jeffers Boney
Margaret H. Booker
Walter Lee Boykins
James A. Braddy
Estelle Murray Brewington

Wayne Dale Brice
Annie Loftin Brown
Hannah Brown
Herman Brown
John B. Brown
Johnnie Brown
Maggie Brown
Mollie G. Brown
Princess Articka D. Brown
Arther Bryant
John Bryant
Lazarus Bryant
Mary D. Bryant
Nancy Boney Bryant
Lina M. Butler
Carolina Carr
Ealie Carr
Edna M. Carr
James E. Carr
Rosa Lee Carr
Thomas E. Carr

Aaron Carroll
Louise Dudley Carter
David F. Chambers
Dinah P. Chambers
Jamima Chambers
Johnnie Chambers
Martha W. Chasten
Thomas Ed Chestnutt
Wicker Coachman
William Corbet
Julia C. Williams Coston
Mary C. Cromartie
Alexander Crumpler
Barbara Ann Crumpler
Hazel Irene Cummings
Katie Dixon
Margaret Dixon
Mattie Dixon
Novie Dixon
John Doe
John Henry Draughan
Moley Evans Dudley
Martha C. Ervin
Beulah Irene Fennell
James C. Fennell
Louanna S. Fennell
Willie C. Fennell
Jannie Fisher
Johnnie Moses Fisher
Catherine V. Flower
Charlie Flowers
William H. Flower
Lizize C. Garner

DUPLIN COUNTY AFRICAN AMERICAN AMERICAN CEMETERIES

Adoram Baptist Church Cemetery
Wallace, North Carolina

Annie Kenan Gavin
Dock Gavin
James Alfonzo Gavin
Lydia Ann Murray Gavin
William Gavin
Susan C. Gorham
Ernestine A. Graham
Buck Grantham
Jaron C. Hall
William Arthur Hall
Bertha F. Hayes
Charles E. Herring
Davetta M. herring
Ellar Herring
Evangeline herring
Frederick S. Herring
Margaret D. Herring
Robert C. Herring
Edmund Highsmith
James High Smith
Odell Highsmith
Russell Frank Hill
Laura Bennet Holmes
Annie Ruth king Horne
Mangle Horne Sr.
Louis C. Houser
David Huffin Jr.
Veenie S. Hyman

Lou Anna Pickett Jackson
Vernia Jane Simmons Jackson
William Jackson
Lendell Davis James
Lennon James
Mary West James
Walter Lee James Sr.
Willie B. James
Mary H. Carr Johnson
Pearcy Johnson
Rita M. Johnson
Alberta B. Jones
Clarence Jones
Dorothy H. Jones
Hattie W. Jones
Lula Jones
David Edward Jordan Sr.
James R. Jordan
Martha Jordan
Mary McMillian Jordan

David Edward Jordan Jr.
Rosa Lee Judge
Annie C. Keith
Catherine S. keith
George E. Keith
George M. Keith
Gladys Lee Mitchell Keith
Henry D. Keith
Leola B. Keith
Nancy keith
Robert Keith Jr.
Samuel Keith
Shaman Keith
Dollie W. Kenan
Elizabeth Kenan
Ernest Kena
Fitzugh Kenan
Georgianna Kenan
Hazel H. Kenan
Irene Graham Kenan
Lionel Kenan
Mary L. Kenan
Sudie Kenan
Walter F. Kenan
Walter F. Kenan
Wilbert T. Kenan
Winifred Nathaniel Kenan
Lucinda Stallings Kidd
Albert G. King
Dorothy M. King
Hattie Louise King
Frances Stallings Lamb
Mary F. Lamb

DUPLIN COUNTY AFRICAN AMERICAN AMERICAN CEMETERIES

Adoram Baptist Church Cemetery
Wallace, North Carolina

Robert Lamb Jr.
Robert Butler Lamb
William Tate Lamb
Ervin Lawery
Alice G. Lawrence
Charlie T. Lawrence
James Lawrence
William R. Lawrence
E D Leonard
James E. Leonard
Naomi M. Leonard
Mattie Lillie
Clodel M. Lowery
Mary J. Lowrie
Lucille M. Mack
Dollie Ann Matthews
Bruce Mathis
Elizabeth P. Mathis
Ethel M. Mathis
Beebell W. Matthews
Connie Matthews
Fitzhugh Matthews Sr.
George W. Matthews
Eunice McAllister
William Edward McCormick
Mary Jane Mcullen
Louis B. McGee
Sidney Thomas McGee
Thomas Henry McGee
Kato McIntire
General McIntyre Jr.
Hubert McIntyre
Elizabeth S. McKenzie
Joe McKenzie Jr.
Jamaica D. McKezee
Bennie McNeill
Berta McMillan
C. W. McMillan
Charles McMillan
Cleacous McMillan
David McMillan
Louise McMillan
Mamie P. McMillan
Oscar McMillan
Peggy Ann McMillan
Rose McMillan
Alice McMillan
Walter C. McMillian
Eaure K. Mellon
Susan M. Mitchell
Charlie Moore
Illa M, Moore
Leroy Vernon Moore
George F. Murphy
Kizzie Murphy
Lucy B. Murphy
Robert Murphy
Robert Murphy
Robert Murphy
Thomas G. Murphy
Dorothy L. Murray
Harvey Murray
James Eustice Murray
John Esau Murray
Liston Murray
Matilda C. Graham Murray
Minnie Tammer Murray
Nicie Mandie Jones Murray
Adeline Gavins Newkirk
Al Smith Newkirk
Amanda Newkirk
Annie C. Bryant Newkirk
Annie P. Newkirk
Beatrice P. Newkirk
Bettie W. Newkirk
Crettie L. Waters Newkirk
Freeman Newkirk
George H. Newkirk
Hattie L. Newkirk
Haywood Newkirk
James Owen Newkrik

DUPLIN COUNTY AFRICAN AMERICAN AMERICAN CEMETERIES

Adoram Baptist Church Cemetery
Wallace, North Carolina

Janie Mae Carter Newkirk
Joseph R. Newkirk
lizzie M. Newkirk
Lou A. Newkirk
Rev. Ludie Newkirk
PFC Morris Henry Newkirk
Phoebe J. Kenan Newkirk
Rosa L. newkirk
Ross Newkirk
Warren Harding Newkirk
Willis Cornelius Newkirk
Annie M. Newkirk
Vanilla Crter Oates
James Daniel Pearsall
Jannie Wells Pearsall
Lillie N. Pearsall
McCoy Pearsall
Daisy Lee Pearsall
Edward Pearson
Luella Peterson
Anna Cooper Pickett
Earl L. Pickett
Nelliw Newton Pickett
William H. Pickett
Alex Pierce
Hattie Davis Peirce
James Andrew Pierce
Mattie N. Pierce

Mildred Powers Pierce
Arletha Kenan Pigford
Annie DeVone Pitts
Alice H. Plummer
Joseph Plummer
Macio Plummer
Robert Plummer Jr.
Robert Plummer Sr.
Roy Plummer
James Powell
Albert Powers Sr.
Annie DeVane Powers
Annie N. Powers
Emanuel T. Powers
James Powers
Walter Powers
John Respir
Henry Lee Rich
Christine W. Robinson
Johnnie Rodgers

John Rogers
Johnnie Rogers
Lina B. Rogers
Hannah J. Rouse
Annie Mae Satchell
Percilla Collern Satchell
Roger Satchell Jr.
Roger Satchell Sr.
Julia Savage
Harriett M. Simmons
Addie Neal Smith
Andrea C. Smith
Bessie M. Smith
Christine Hill Smith
Mimia W. Smith
Robert Lee Smith
Robert Lee Smith Jr.
Catherine DeVane Stallings
Florence Stallings
Henry Stallings
john J. Stallings
Lucie Stallings
Pearlie Riles
Queen Corbett Stallings
Roosevelt Stallings
soloman Stallings
Annie Ruth Stevens
Callie T. Stevens
Hannah Stevens
Mandy Stevens
Mollie Boney Stevens
Nancy A. Stevens

182

DUPLIN COUNTY AFRICAN AMERICAN AMERICAN CEMETERIES

Adoram Baptist Church Cemetery
Wallace, North Carolina

Duke Street
Oscar Stringfield
Charles Stukes
Cleo Stukes
Grant Stukes
Lee D. Stukes
Mary J. Stukes
Robert Lee Stukes
Clyde Teachy
Edith Teachy
Lizzie Teachy
Philimore Teachy
Shirley Dail Teachy
Dora Thomas
Sidney Thomas Jr.
Mamie G. Thompson
Arthur C. Usher
Lelar Usher
Sarah E. Usher
Elama Boney Wade
Bertha Wallace
Edna H. Wallace
John D. Wallace
Luther C. Wallace
Cora N. Waters
Elizabeth Waters
Samuel Waters
Frances M. Watkins

Oscar E. Watkins
Darlene Yvette James Webster
Bettie Wells
Carrie Wells
Dave Wells
F. E. Wells
Harry Wells
Harry Lee Wells
Laura Wells
Lee Wells
Linda Kaye Brice Wells
Vallie M. Wells
W. T. Wells
George W. Wiggins
Mattie K. Wiggins
Richard Wiggins
Benjamin Williams
Carl U. Williams
Glennie C. Williams
Leo Williams

Marginia West Williams
Mary Eveline Williams
Rosa Ann Williams
Thomas Henry Williams
Ella W. Willis
Pearlie Willis
Rosie Belle White
Elizabeth W. Wilson
Granger l. Wilson
Herman Wilson
Herman Wilson
lewis E. Woods
Charles E. Wright
Cleo Wright
Gertrude M. Wright
Gladys Wright
James Lamon Wright
Maggie Mable Wright
Timothy T. Wright

DUPLIN COUNTY AFRICAN AMERICAN AMERICAN CEMETERIES

Fennel Family Cemetery
Kenansville, North Carolina

Ethel J. Fennell
William R. Fennell

DUPLIN COUNTY AFRICAN AMERICAN AMERICAN CEMETERIES

Arthur Graham Cemetery
Kenansville, North Carolina

Luberta Dixon
Annnie Mae Graham Dobson
Lannie Bell Graham
Cocero C. Graham
Mary Malisa Graham
Pummie S. Graham
Arthur Graham
Ralph Bernard Hall Sr.
Arthenta C. HallJ
Jannie M. Hall
George Hall
Sonia D. Middleton

DUPLIN COUNTY AFRICAN AMERICAN AMERICAN CEMETERIES

Curtis Farrior Cemetery
Kenansville, North Carolina

Felix Boney
Atha Farrior
Curtis Farrior
James Edward Farrior Jr.
Mark C. Farrior
Mary E. Farrior
Mary H. Farrior
Percy David Farrior
Alberta Farrior Monk
Effie Monk
Gaynell Monk
Tommie Bailey Monk
Thomas Monk Jr.

DUPLIN COUNTY AFRICAN AMERICAN AMERICAN CEMETERIES

Miller Cemetery
Kenansville, North Carolina

Alberta M. Barden
Gerald Amos Barden
James Herman Barden
Leslie Barden Jr.
Valerie O. Barden
Vernal Barden
Roberta Boney
Stella Maxine Brooks
Chaelene Brooks Faison
Lula I. Hardy
Will Jarman
James Johnson
Chelsey Kelly
Willis M. King
Rebecca D. McIver
Mary M. McKiver
Arminda Lessane Miller
Baby Girl Miller
Baby Girl Miller
Barbara A. Dixon Miller

Beulah Miller
Bryant D. Miller
Charlie Miller
Charlie Miller Jr.
Clara Lou Miller
Daren Lamar Miller
Freeman Miller Jr.
Gregory Miller
Hazel Miller
Isaac Miller Jr.
James Garfield Miller
James E Miller
Jimmie Miller
Joseph H. Miller
Larry N. Miller
Matthew D. Miller
Martha M. Miller
Marie Ann Miller
Mary E. Miller
O'Berry Miller

Roger D. Miller
Norris J. Murphy
Arthur D. Quinn
Norman S. Savage
Daisy C. Sharpless
Annie G. Smith
Coy C. Smith
Coy P. Smith
Hettie J. Smith
Macy Miller Smith
Richard L. Smith
Susie A. Smith
Thomas O. Smith
Namond D. Wallace
Sue M. Wallace

DUPLIN COUNTY AFRICAN AMERICAN AMERICAN CEMETERIES

Shaw Temple AME Zion Church Cemetery
Magnolia, North Carolina

Lela Shaw Boney Ashford
Fronie Carroll Barden
Daughter Barden
Allen Earl Barnes
Isaac Batts
James Batts
Margarett Elizabeth Dickerson Batts
Rose Annie McFarland Batts
Lessie Beatty
Neil Beatty III
Ruthie Bethune
Cora A Robinson Boney
Earl Boney
Fannie Southerland Boney
Harford Earl Boney
Holland Boney
James Alvin Boney
Juanita Boney
Lizzie Sheffield Boney
Marjorie Savage Boney
Raymond Boney
Robert Horace Boney

Rosa Bell Whitehead Boney
Sidney Theodore Boney
Addie L. Boney Brown
Albert Scott Brown
Cora Bell Brown
Eddie D. Brown
Elton C. Brown
Henry Thomas Brown
Herminia Brown
Infant Daughter Brown
Irving E. Brown
Lula Jane Korngay Briwn
Neady Viola Pickett Brown
Raymond C. Brown
Walter Lee Brown
Willie P. Brown
Dolph Bryant
Rossie Mae Carr Bryant
Sarah Bryant
Willie James Bryant

Adline Carr
Chancey J. Carr
Elizabeth Bradshaw Carr
Fannie B. Carroll Carr
Jacob Carr
James H. Carr
James O. Carr
Jimmie L. Carr
Leatha A. Monroe Carr
Margie Anna Brown Carr
Zebulon Vander Carr
Addie Florence Parker Carroll
Corp Albert Lee Carroll
Andrew Carroll
Annie Carroll
Annie Bell Carroll
Bert Carroll
Bert Carroll Jr.
Bobby Carroll
Demasko Carroll
Florence Hazel Carroll
Fonnie Carroll Jr.
Gladys Carroll

DUPLIN COUNTY AFRICAN AMERICAN AMERICAN CEMETERIES

Shaw Temple AME Zion Church Cemetery
Rose Hill, North Carolina

Gregory M. Carroll
Hannah Carroll
James A. Carroll Jr.
Jim Carroll
John D. Carroll
Kary Carroll
Lottie O. Carroll
Mamie C. Carroll
Martha Carroll
Maxie Carroll
Mima Ludell Hall carroll
Rachel O. Carroll
Robert L. Carroll
Solon Carroll
Tommie Carroll
Willie Lee Carroll
Henrietta J. Carter
Sherman Carter
Wilma Murphy Carter
Agnes Ruth Dixon Chasten
Cornell Chasten
Deanna D. Chasten
Denise M. Chasten

Eric Terrell Chasten
Eunice M. Chasten
Henry Chasten Sr.
M. Henry Chasten
Monique LaCarol Chasten
Mozell Chasten
Rena Barden Chasten
Theodore Chasten
Luberta Jones Collins
Mattie Carroll Coston
Alberta Powell Council
Purvis D. Council
Cora Carroll Daniels
Annie Frances Batts Dixon
Clarence Dixon
D. Wright Dixon
Fannie Bell Murphy Dixon
Jessie Southerland Dixon
Sgt. Juno Lasale Dixon
Kathern Dixon

Leno M. Dixon
Sarah S. Dixon
William C. Dixon
Willie David Dixon
Allie Carroll Dobson
Harry Lee Dobson
Baby Daughter Dobson
Perry Lee Dobson
Willie C. Dobson
Gloria Dean Drake
Bill Ellis
Peggy Dixon Ellis
Verta Mae Flowers
Gwyn Whitney Frederick Sr.
Margie Boney Frederick
Mamie Ruth Dixon Glasper
Walter James Glasper
Baby Boy Hall
Lossie Lee Gardner hall
Earl Hartford
Fannie Southerland Hartford
John B. Houston
Leatha Ruth Dixon Houston

DUPLIN COUNTY AFRICAN AMERICAN AMERICAN CEMETERIES

Shaw Temple AME Zion Church Cemetery
Rosehill, North Carolina

Gail J. Howard
James G. Howard
Carrie Mae Middleton James
Eugenia Carroll James
Nathaniel James
Richard James
Roosevelt James
Walter James
Warren G. James
Dwight Johnson
Henry Clay Jones
Priscilla Jones
Robert Jones
Rev. Leslie Kelly
Mattie James Kelly
Donald Ray Kenan
Annie Mae Dixon Kenion
Hary Lee Kenion
Laura Ann Kenion
Hary Lee Kenion Jr.
Alexander Kornegay Sr.
Charlie Kornegay
Clara Kornegay
John P. Lanier
Mora S. Lanier
Alexander Leach Jr.
Mary Lillie Brown Mallard
David Mathis Jr.
Wilma G. Matthews
Rudolph McClain
Malakia Jannie McCullough
Brenda Faye McGee
Roy Gene McGee
Andonia K. Middleton
PFC Lester Middleton
Annie Lois Murphy
Benjamin F. Murphy
Charlie Davis Murphy
Geraldine Cooper Murphy
Lula Exum Murphy
Malcy L. Murphy
Mary Eloise Murphy
Ransom Levi Murphy
Bernice Boney Newkirk
Gordon Newkirk
Ocea Maxine Council Newkirk
Patricia Ann Outlaw
Julis O. Picket
Hezekiah Shaw
Benton L. Sheffield
Polly Jane Boney Sheffield
Sanders Sheffield
Sarah W. Carroll Sloan
Alice Smith
Alma Boney Smith
Richard F. Smith
Richard Hansley Smith
Robert Edward Smith
William Henry Smith
Emma Dixon Stokes
Haywood Teachy
Andrew Jabari Washington
Alice Marie Murphy Williams
Andria Shyann Williams
Edwina Williams

DUPLIN COUNTY AFRICAN AMERICAN AMERICAN CEMETERIES

Dudley Monk Cemetery
Kenansville, North Carolina

Armite Carlton
Gladys M. Hardy
Jimmie D. Hooks
Edd Dudley Monk
James D. Monk
Johnnie F. Monk
Johnnie McD Monk
Lucille S. Monk
Marie Allen Monk
Martha S. Monk

Mattie Southerland Monk
Robert Edward Monk
William D. Monk
William McKinley Monk
Catonda G. Smith
Ellomethia D. Smith
Jessie N. Smith Sr.
Thaddeus Williams

DUPLIN COUNTY AFRICAN AMERICAN AMERICAN CEMETERIES

Boyette Family Cemetery
Bowden Cemetery

Amy Boyette
Anna Mae Bowden Boyette
Julia R. Hill Boyette
Kathleen Boyette
Owen Boyette
Rev. Adam J. Carlton
Mahalia Boyette Carlton
Pleasant Boyette Hodges
Squire Hodges

DUPLIN COUNTY AFRICAN AMERICAN AMERICAN CEMETERIES

Hallsville Missionary Baptist Church Cemetery
Hallsville, North Carolina

Vernetter J. Batts
King Soloman Batts Sr.
Marcus Bradshaw
Maggie M. Hall Brinson
Matthew Brinson
William J. Brinson
William S. Brinson
Annie E. Britt
Julius H. Britt
Elisha Brown
Genevia Brown
James Dudley Brown
Lula Lenix Brown
Troy Ray Brown
Carson D. Bryant
Fred Bryant
Louis Bryant
Sylvia Bryant
Sherman Burgess
Noah Burnett
Verline H. Burnett
Evelyn F. Burnette
Reba Leverne Carter
Thelma P. Chasten
George L. Cooper
Spicey JaneCooper
William B. Cooper

Edna Davis
Hilda G. Davis
Lela D. Davis
Noah Davis
Robert Davis
Robert J. Davis
Sula Mae Farland Davis
Wade James Davis
Willie C. Davis
James A. Deaver
James R. Deaver
Roland Deaver
Rudolph Deaver
Sarah H. Deaver
Bertha H. Deavers
N. L. Dobson
Lula Lee Doss

Eugene Farrior
Frances Farrior
Geraldine D. Farrior
Gladys M. Farrior
Jerry Farrior
John E. Farrior
Johnnie W. Farrior
Lacy Farrior
Richard Farrior
Thomas G. Farrior
William R. J. Farrior
Robert Furlow
Ada M. Hall
Addie D. Hall
Alee E. Hall
Bonnie Henry Hall
Cora Hall
David J. Hall

Katie B. Hall
Lil Hall
Lillie B. Hall
Lillie M. Hall
Lizzie Hall
Louis N. Hall
Marcella Hall
Marshall Edward Hall
Martha Ann Hall
Mary J. Hall
Mary L. Dobson Hall
Raymond N. Hall
Ruby G. Hall
Tommie Ray Hall
William E. Hall
Larry Allen Highsmith
Bonie Henry Hill
Helen Winley Ingram
H. James
Donna B. Jarmon
Bettie J. Kelly
Debrow Kelly
Edward Lee Kelly
James E. Lanier
Lillian G. Lanier
Mary E. Lucus

DUPLIN COUNTY AFRICAN AMERICAN AMERICAN CEMETERIES

Farrior -Moore Cemetery
Kenansville, North Carolina

Samuel B. Lucus
Gertrude B. Mallard
James Mallard
James Colden McAllister
Mary Magdalene McAllister
Deloras M. H. McGowan
Lillie Ruth Miller
Charlie J. Murphy
Hallie Murphy
Katie J. Murphy
William H. Murphy
Rosella Outlaw
Adell H. Parker
David Parker
Josephine Whitehead Parker
Matho Parker
Callie M. Pearsall
Johnny F. Pearsall
Lillie Mae Pearsall
Frank Pearsall
Eddie Pearsall
Charlie Powers
Margie Powers
Willie Pridgen
Marria Riley
James H. Simmons Jr.
Mary E. Simmons
Tom Southerland
Lazarus Spencer
Louise Spencer
Hattie P. Stallings
Joe Louis Stallings
Jacqueline F. Still
William James Stroud
Reba Ward
Amos J. Whitehead
Ardelia Williams
Beverly Williams
Bryant E. Williams
Cassie M. Williams
Cecelia F. Williams
Charlie GreenWilliams
Charlie Williams Jr.
Delois M. Williams
Dock Williams
Easter B. Williams
Ella J. Williams
Emma M. Williams
Eugene Williams Sr.
John R. Williams
Laddie Williams
Lola B. Williams
Lossie Williams
Lude Williams
Marie M. Williams
Mary K. Williams
Pearl V. Williams
Tom Williams
Willie L. Williams
Florida E. Winley
Gary Winley
Leroy W. Winley
Rev. James Roy Winley
Savannah E. Winley

DUPLIN COUNTY AFRICAN AMERICAN AMERICAN CEMETERIES

Hill Cemetery
Lyman, North Carolina

Toyie B. Hill
Vernell Hill

DUPLIN COUNTY AFRICAN AMERICAN AMERICAN CEMETERIES

Hall Cemetery
Beulaville, North Carolina

Maggie Carr
Ada Carr Hall
Annie Hall
Onnie C. Hall
Robert Hall
Samuel Hall
Zoye Hall
Johnnie Stallings
Jimmie Lee Williams
Minnnie Iola Williams

DUPLIN COUNTY AFRICAN AMERICAN AMERICAN CEMETERIES

Chestnut-Dixon Cemetery
Magnolia, North Carolina

Rena Dixon Best
Ivory L. Chestnut
Samuel Chestnutt
Sedell D. Crawford
Rev. Willie L. Dixon
Katie Ree Wadsworth

DUPLIN COUNTY AFRICAN AMERICAN AMERICAN CEMETERIES

Williams Family Cemetery
Magnolia, North Carolina

Marie Harrison
Charlie M. Williams
Harvey Lee Williams
Ida M. Williams
James E. Williams
Louise Williams

DUPLIN COUNTY AFRICAN AMERICAN AMERICAN CEMETERIES

Branch Cemetery
Albertson, North Carolina

Christopher A. Bizzell
Doris Branch Bizzell
Elaine Olive Bizzell
Corp. Vance Oliver Bizzell
Alton R. Branch
Baby Branch
Clifton Andrew Branch
Flora Miller Branch
Gaston Branch
Gaston Branch Jr.
Gaston D. Branch IV
James T. Branch
Leslie Branch
Leslie Branch Jr.
Levie Branch
Mae V. G. Branch
Mary Lee Davis Branch
Minnie Branch
Raymond Earl Branch
Winston L. Branch
Orieton E. Houston
Jessie James Jones
Pearlie Mae Branch Korneygay
Earl Moore Jr.
Sauquan Sabastian Sharpe

DUPLIN COUNTY AFRICAN AMERICAN AMERICAN CEMETERIES

Southerland Cemetery
Kenansville, North Carolina

Beatrice Dixon
Charles M. Dixon
Council Dixon Jr.
Edna S. Dixon
F Council Dixon
Sherman L. Dixon
Mildred Ray S. Graham
Bertha Lee Kenan
Cornelius Southerland
Lila Southerland
Liston Southerland
Matthew J. Southerland
Matthew Southerland
Mattie Dobson Southerland
Myrtle Lee Southerland
O'Neal Southerland
Robert M. Southerland
Thelma D Southerland

DUPLIN COUNTY AFRICAN AMERICAN AMERICAN CEMETERIES

Jones Chapel Church Cemetery
Beulaville, North Carolina

Baby Boy Brinson
Orpha L. Jones Brinson
Clark Muriel Chasten
Ida Jane Jones Chasten
Rannie Lou Chasten
Thomas Henry Chasten
Mary E. Jones Henderson
Johnny T. Highsmith
Brenda Farrior Holmes
Amos B. Jones
Ernestine Jones
Estella Miller Jones
Joel Jones
John Henry Jones Jr.
Leah Jane Hall Jones
William R. Jones
Alberta L. Miller
Zollie Haywood Pickett
Ida Mae Pigford
Robin Roby
Edwina Lee Suggs
Roberta Deloris Suggs
Percy Wilkins
PFC John Henry Williams
Verneel S. Stokes Williams

DUPLIN COUNTY AFRICAN AMERICAN AMERICAN CEMETERIES

Daisy's Chapel Cemetery
Beulaville, North Carolina

Allie V. Boyette
Adolph Branch
Franklin Boyette
Mary Branch
Ophelia T. Brown
Rashaan Carroll
Bertha Chasten Maddox
Dorothy T. Chasten
Gerald D. Maddox
Eva Graham Chasten
Maggie M. Chasten
Martha Graham Chasten
Tom I. Chasten
Walter Bryant Chasten
Clara M. Collins
Ethel M. Cooper
John U. Cooper Sr.
Alvin Louise Evans Dixon
Gorden D. Dobson
Katie L. Dobson
Katie Gordon Dobson
Mary Gladys Pitts Crew
Mary A. Evans
Viola M. Evans
Olivia Edwards
James A. Evans Sr.
James C. Evans
Robert A. Evans
Eddie J. Geigher
Laura Geigher
Lura J. Geigher
Carrie C. Graham
Lassie B. Green
Mildred C. Green
Quincy S. Green
Johnny T. Highsmith
Brenda Farrior Holmes
Jaeanette Chasten Humphrey
Sarah E. Jones
Betty Dorothy Maddox
Minerva R. McBryde
Wilma Monroe
Cleveland R. Parker
Ethro Parker
Etta Viel Parker
Hinkley Parker
James K. Parker
Katie I. Graham Parker
Leonard Parker
Luther C. Parker
Williby Parker
William Parker
Virile L. Perkins
Lawanda Pickett
Ada B. Pitts
OFC Boas Lewely Pitts
Erma Lee Pitts
Lorienser Parker
Edna H. Savage
Bernice Leatrice Suggs

DUPLIN COUNTY AFRICAN AMERICAN AMERICAN CEMETERIES

Williams Cemetery
Summerlins Crossroads- Kenansville, North Carolina

Cassie Ann William Smith
Estelle O. Smith
George P. Smith
Kater Smith
Theordic Talmage Smith
Caroline Pearsall
Anthony D. Williams Sr.
George D. Williams
Dundee R. Williams
Eddie J. Williams
James Andrew Williams
Mary Lillie Pettiford Williams
Willie Williams

DUPLIN COUNTY AFRICAN AMERICAN AMERICAN CEMETERIES

Dixon Cemetery
Kenansville, North Carolina

Philathead D. Allen
Bruce Dixon Jr.
Bruce Dixon Sr.
Daniel Dixon
Grace Elizabeth Dixon
James David Dixon
Mattie Mae Smith Dixon
Mary Lillie Wells Highsmith
Daisey Bell James Wells
Simon Roscoe Wells

DUPLIN COUNTY AFRICAN AMERICAN AMERICAN CEMETERIES

Carr Family Cemetery
Mount Olive, North Carolina

Anna Brinson Artis
Robert Artis
Fannie Carr Bass
Cora Lee Carlton
Essie Louise Carr Carlton
Levi Carlton
Margaret Lee Carr Carlton
Addie Carr
Alethia Boney Carr
Benjamin Carr
Charlie Carr
Earl Carr

Ellen Olive Carr
Geneva Murray Carr
James Dixon
Estelle Pettiford Hart
Joseph Pettiford
Joshua Pettiford
Lizzie Robinson
Dora Williams
Lillie May Williams
Oscar Williams
Rob Williams

DUPLIN COUNTY AFRICAN AMERICAN AMERICAN CEMETERIES

Brinson Cemetery
Kenansville, North Carolina

Charlie Earl Brinson
John Thomas Brinson
Martha L. Brinson
Mary Helen Brinson
Jessie Coleman
Lucille Coleman
Lucy C. Pearsall
James H. Sanders
Mary L. Sanders

DUPLIN COUNTY AFRICAN AMERICAN AMERICAN CEMETERIES

Brinson Cemetery
Kenansville, North Carolina

Alexander Brinson
Bernice Brinson
Brindon Anthony Brinson
Christopher Brinson
Davie J. Brinson
Eva Lee Brinson
James H. Brinson Sr.
Louella S. Brinson
Maggie B. Brinson
Marenda Brinson
Roy Brinson
Carrie L. Brunson
John H. Brunson
Rosie Campbell Brunson
Leo B. Bryant
Delia B. Lofton
Joseph Loften
Essie P. Moore
Jacqueline V. Smith
Juanita B. Young

DUPLIN COUNTY AFRICAN AMERICAN AMERICAN CEMETERIES

Stanford Cemetery
Kenansville, North Carolina

Hattie Stanford Fisher
Allen P. Moore
Carrie Murphy Moore
John A. Moore
Johnie E. Moore
Leah S. Moore
Mary Moore
Solomom W. Moore
Willie Lavonsa Moore
Willie Moore Jr.
Annie Pollock
Annie S. Roberts
Annie B. Stanford
George Stanford

DUPLIN COUNTY AFRICAN AMERICAN AMERICAN CEMETERIES

Kenan Cemetery
Kenansville, North Carolina

Mary Middleton Basden
Eddie Bryant
Ruth Phillips Bryant
Herman Cooper
Clarence Faison Sr.
Rene P. Faison
Lewis Nick Hall
Arthur Dan Hebron
Lila Kenan Hebron
Kirmey Kenan
Luella Underwood Kenan
Robert Kenan
Thelma J. Kenan
Rev. Willie G. Kenan

Wayne Kenan
Abb Phillips
Minnie Phillips
Owen Phillips
Roy L. Phillip
Danette Smith Morrisey
Elmore Middleton
George Luther Middleton Sr.
Gary R. Wiggins
Valarie J. Wiggins
Leroy Wiggins
Minnie P. Wiggins
Milton Wiggins
Vincent Wiggins

DUPLIN COUNTY AFRICAN AMERICAN AMERICAN CEMETERIES

Graham Chapel Cemetery
Kenansville, North Carolina

Arthur Fullwood
Hannah Louise Houston Fullwood
Prentice Fullwood
Alvin R. Graham
Catherine Graham
Rev. Cleveland Graham
Doretha R. Graham
Evelyn Graham
Johnnie Graham
Joseph E. Graham
Hannah M. Graham
Rev. Hardy Graham
Roy Lee Graham
James Edward Hill
Jessie R. Hill
Sandra Gail Hill
Sarah J. Hill
Wayne Hill
Levon Houston
Mary Bell Houston

Durwood G. Graham
Mary Graham
Rev. R. Vann Graham
Joyce H. Pigford
Donald C. Miller
Donal O'Harrell Miller
George Miller Jr.
Johnnie Miller
Johnnie R. Miller
Mable Miller
Martha G. Miller
Mildred Miller
N. Jae E. Miller
Perry Gene Miller
Robert L. Miller
Sylvester Miller
Willie Mae Miller
Aaron J. Newkirk
Mariah J. Newkirk
Willie G Newkirk
Jimmy E. Smith

DUPLIN COUNTY AFRICAN AMERICAN AMERICAN CEMETERIES

Pickett Cemetery
Chinquapin, North Carolina

James White Jr.
Elizabeth J. White
Mariah Judge
Alexander Judge
Alexander Judge Sr.
Ronald L. Sharpless
Donald Lee Sharpless
Rev. Alfred Sharpless
Henry F. Lee
Vena G. Lee
Margaret Judge
Liston Judge
Mary Cassie Judge
Hulan O. Pickett
Terrence D. Pickett

Quintelia Lee Gore
Annie B. Hartley
Frederick Lee
Edmond W. Lee
Sylvia C. Lee
Eric Leroy Pickett
Mary Bella Pcikett
Herny Lee Judge
Fannie L. Judge
Roosevelt L. Pickett
Eliza Jane Lee Pickett
Will M. Pickett
Eulah Pickett
Elder Arto Pickett
Preston Elijah Pickett

DUPLIN COUNTY AFRICAN AMERICAN AMERICAN CEMETERIES

Stokes Cemetery
Magnolia, North Carolina

Adelaide Stokes
Arthur Stokes
Edward Stokes
Hettie Wells Stokes
James E. Stokes
Katie Stokes
Rev. Warrick Stokes

DUPLIN COUNTY AFRICAN AMERICAN AMERICAN CEMETERIES

Graham- Boney Cemetery
Greenevers, North Carolina

Keith Abram
Rivers R. Blakes
Elliott Boney
Frances Boney
John T. Boney
Julia Ann Boney
Norman W. Boney
Sprunt Boney
Susan Ann McGee Boney
Susan Nan Boney
Walter D. Boney
Walter Boney Jr.
William H. Boney
Rosa Lee Bradshaw
John B. Carr

Dudley Dixon
Purley Dixon
Laura B. Dunn
Pattie Peterson Hayes
Abbie Chasten Herring
William H. Herring
Florence Faulkner
James Graham
James Dudley Graham
Sarah Graham
Ader Dixon McFlecther
Vassie Herring Middleton
Henry Moore Jr.
Henry Steven Moore
George H. Williams

DUPLIN COUNTY AFRICAN AMERICAN AMERICAN CEMETERIES

James Thomas Moore Family Cemetery
Kenansville, North Carolina

Bernice Loftin Moore
Clarence Earl Moore Sr.
James Thomas Moore Jr.
Pamela C. Murphy

DUPLIN COUNTY AFRICAN AMERICAN AMERICAN CEMETERIES

Swaney Field Cemetery
Chinquapin North Carolina

Nola Pickett Bardon
Frances Maylord Pickett Corbett
Katie Ardesia Corbett
Lula Clyde Newkirk Hall
Jermima Graham Judge
Luberta Kelly
Albert L. Pickett
Anna Belle Newkirk Pickett
Caleb Cail Pickett
Chelsia Kenan Pickett
Daniel R. Pickett
Hannah Evelina Wells Pickett
Julia Stokes Pickett
Marinda Becton Pickett
Rayfield Robert Pickett
Roscoe Pickett
Silas Pickett

DUPLIN COUNTY AFRICAN AMERICAN AMERICAN CEMETERIES

Davis Family Cemetery
Albertson, North Carolina

Lillie Belle Brown
Will Brown
Albert Davis
Any Ann Davis
Angelane Davis
Beulah M. Davis
Commie D. Davis
Douglass A. Davis
Emeline Davis
Harriett Davis
Henry T. Davis
Hiram Davis
Katherleen Davis
Kellie C. Davis
Kelly R. Davis
Lannie Davis
lenzie S. Davis
Mary S. Davis

Mozella Davis
Myrtice P. Davis
Rivers Davis
Robert E. Davis
William Authur Davis
York Davis
Rufus E. Davis
Sallie W. Davis
Sarah E. Davis
Timothy M. Davis
Addie Lee Davis Garner
Perla A. Jarman
David Lee Jenkins
Cloe Ann Smith
Leroy smith
Rebecca D. Smith
Ruben Smith
Sherman J. Smith

DUPLIN COUNTY AFRICAN AMERICAN AMERICAN CEMETERIES

Brinson Cemetery
Kenansville, North Carolina

Baby Brinson
Addie Pearl Brinson
Amos Jones Brinson
Annie Irene Brinson
Ashley Graham Brinson
Alexander Brinson
Bernice Brinson
Brandon Anthony Brinson
Christopher R. Brinson
Cora E. Bostic Brinson
David J. Brinson
Eleanor Louise Brinson
Emma Brock Brinson
Eva Lee Brinson
Florence A. Teachey Brinson
Henry Brinson
Hiram Jones Brinson
Infant Boy Brinson
Infant Brinson
Infant Boy Brinson
Infant Boy Brinson
Infant Girl Brinson
Infant Girl Brinson
Irene Williams Brinson
Jessie Brown Brinson

John Henry Brinson
John William Brinson
Katie Davis Southerland Brinson
Leroy Hiram Brinson
Lester Stewart Brinson
Louella Savage Brinson
Maggie L. Bryant Brinson
Marenda Brinson
Martha Jane Goodman Brinson
Mary Ellen Bostic Brinson
Rosie Lee Campbell Brinson
Roy Brinson
Carrie Lee Brunson
James Henry Brunson
Decatur Bryant Jr.
Fred Bryant
Katie Mae Bryant
Leo B. Bryant
Oppie Bryant
Eva Brinson Blanton Hughes
Joseph Loftin
Delia Brinson Lofton
Essie Pearl Brinson Moore
Jacqueline V. Smith
Juanita Brinson Young

DUPLIN COUNTY AFRICAN AMERICAN AMERICAN CEMETERIES

Rainbow Cemetery
Kenansville, North Carolina

James Best
Tuby B. Best
Lanyia Monique Best
Arnold B. Best
Classie Brinson
Everett Brinson
jessie J. Brinson
Johnnie F. Brinson
Larry Donnell Brinson
Martha S. Brinson
Milton D. Brinson
Leroy Bryant
Leroy Bryant Jr.
Willie Dell Moore Bryant
Beverly A. Butler
Mable L. Butler
Beulah Edwards
donald Ray Edwards
Joan Edwards
Eillie L. Edwards Jr.
Ada M. Faison

Johnnie E. Faison
Charlie Glaspie
Curtis W. Glaspie
Helen Glaspie
Henry Glaspie
Herbert R. Glaspie
James O. Glaspie
Lonnie W. Glaspie
Rosa L. Glaspie
William F. Glaspie
Dennis Herrington
Reynolds Hills
Darius Hodges
Jartavius T. Hodges
Mary L. Hodges
Michael D. Hodges
Herman Houston
Roberta E. Houston
Ernestine M. Kea
Luvenia F. Kea
H. B. Kornegay

Lillie Ruth Kornegay
Geneva B. Miller
Charlie Moore
Lucy Moore
Bobby Nickleson
Homer Nickelson
Katie Lee Nickelson
Margaret Nickelson
James T. Pearsall
James E. Pickett
Lenora W. Royal
Leona Stokes
Leroy Whitfiled Sr.
John H. Williams
Ozella Williams

DUPLIN COUNTY AFRICAN AMERICAN AMERICAN CEMETERIES

Burton Cemetery
Deep Bottom, North Carolina

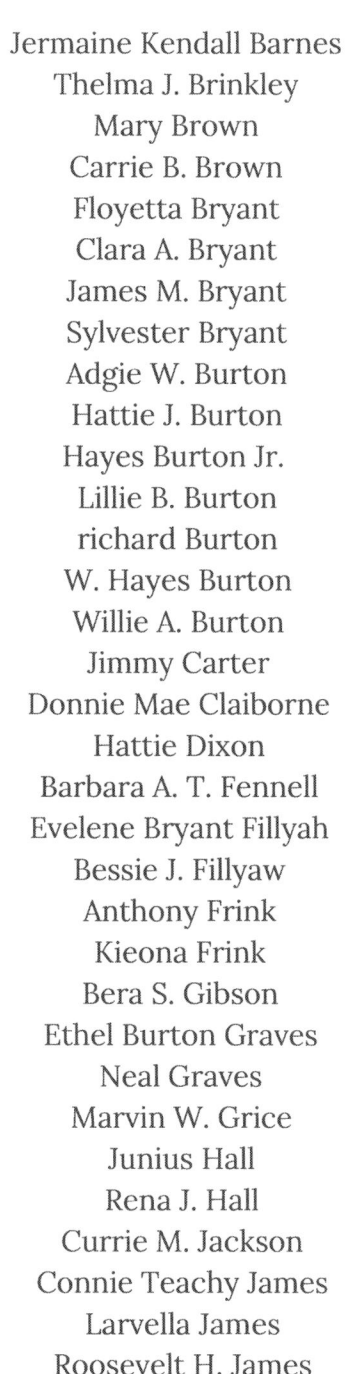

Jermaine Kendall Barnes
Thelma J. Brinkley
Mary Brown
Carrie B. Brown
Floyetta Bryant
Clara A. Bryant
James M. Bryant
Sylvester Bryant
Adgie W. Burton
Hattie J. Burton
Hayes Burton Jr.
Lillie B. Burton
richard Burton
W. Hayes Burton
Willie A. Burton
Jimmy Carter
Donnie Mae Claiborne
Hattie Dixon
Barbara A. T. Fennell
Evelene Bryant Fillyah
Bessie J. Fillyaw
Anthony Frink
Kieona Frink
Bera S. Gibson
Ethel Burton Graves
Neal Graves
Marvin W. Grice
Junius Hall
Rena J. Hall
Currie M. Jackson
Connie Teachy James
Larvella James
Roosevelt H. James
Stacy James
Jessie L. Judge
Mattie Teachy Judge
Melinda M. Judge
Roy Henry Judge
Cardelia McNeal
Beatrice Middleton
Johnnie Mitchel
Donald R. Morrisey
Evelyn Parks
Neomia S. Pickett
Beatrice Poindexter
Nancy A. Judge Reddick
Juanita B. Robinson
Sallie Kenon Savage
James H. Scarborough
Ashley Scarborough Jr.
Lenell Scarborough
Mable K. Scarborough
Martha L. Scarborough
Lenell Scarborough
Mable K. Scarborough
Martha L. Scarborough
Queen Scarborough
Sebron M. Scarborough
Ward Scarborough
Willie L. Scarborough
Curtis Spearman
Gertrude Spearman
Hettie M. Spearman
Emanuel Spearman Jr.
Emanuel Spearman Sr.
Nancy Ann Spearman
Rodolph Spearman
Sallie Ann Spearman
Welsey Spearman
Willie W> Spearman
Erie Taylor
James Taylor
John W. Taylor
Mary Virginia Taylor
Richard Taylor
Edroe Teachey
John E. Teachey
Mary S. Teachey
William H. Teachey
Charlie McNeal Thomas
Georgia P. Thomas
Robert Thomas Jr.
Lizzie J. Thomas
Mamie B. Whitehead
Davis B. Williams
Willie J. Williams

DUPLIN COUNTY AFRICAN AMERICAN AMERICAN CEMETERIES

Rockfish AME Church Cemetery
Wallace, North Carolina

Jake Andrews
Josh May Banks
Josephone Carter Barden
Willie J. Beamon
Mary P. Blount
Sam Blount
Sam Blount
Easter Boney
Easter Boney
Felix Boney
Frances A. Boney
Frances Boney
Johnny I. Boney
Malissie F. J. Boney
Nancy E. Boney
Waymond Boney
Dilcy Bryant
John William Byrant
Laura Bryant
Vernette M. Bryant
Walter K. Bryant
Edward L. Carr
Jack Carr
Levi Nixon. Carr
Mary L. Carr
Carrie M Hall Carter
Darryl Peace Carter
Dennis Terell Carter
James Tyrone Carter
Linwood Carter
Betsy O. Casey

Mattie Lee Clibbons
Muriel D. Coston
Rena L. Murray Crumpler
Mary Love Daniels
Lillie H. Davis
Willie Carroll Dixon
Carolyn A. Evans
Evelyn N Farrior
Patience Ford
Lucretia M. Franklin
Georgia Carter Goodson
Aaron Gray
Elizabeth E. Gray
Dollie Williams Hand
James D. Hand
Bernice Harrison
Crettie L. Hatten
Bertha T. Henderson
Lloyd D. Henry
Andrew Herring

Thomas S. Herring
Clifton Highsmith
Eddie Highsmith
Louise M. Highsmith
Rita J. Highsmith
Olivia N. James
Sears James Sr.
Dawson Jordan
Gene Gregory Jordan
James R. Jordan
Mary A. Jordan
Rosa Bell Jordan
William E. Jordan
Annie Lawery
Cora Lawrence Jr.
Willie Mae Lawrence
Annie Julia Love
Charlie Love
Iola Murphy Love
Jimmy Love
Julia J. Love
Lee Davis Love
Willie Lowe
Lillie Love Mathis
Lois S. Matthews
Lucile W. McCoy
Gloria W. McKenzie
Mae G. McMillan

DUPLIN COUNTY AFRICAN AMERICAN AMERICAN CEMETERIES

Farrior Cemetery
Kenansville, North Carolina

Calvin Baker
Arthur T. Boney
Joe Louis Boney
John D. Boney
Lula B. Boney
Retha Mae Estella Boney
Sherman Boney
T. R. Boney
W. R. Boney
Ora C. Boone
Sanders Boone
James A. Bryant
Maggie Bryant
Curtis Farrior
Estella B. Farrior
George T. Farrior
George W. Farrior
Kimberly Fontaine Farrior
Leslie Mae Farrior
Robert L. Farrior
Katherine Frederick
Allen Herring
Crettie M. Herring
Georgia E. Herring
Pearlie Herring
Stephen Herring
Kendra L. Hodges
Lakendra Keshay Hodges
Alexandra Cheri Jackson
Retra M. Jackson
Mary E. Jarman
Needham B. Jarman Sr.
Ashaya S. McGowan
Pamelia W. Middleton
Albert L. Moore
Audrey F. Moore
Cheryl F. Moore
Claudie W. Moore
David Moore
David Moore Jr.
Mary L. Monk
Oscar L. Moore
Renee Moore
Timothy Moore
Joyce Ann Pickett
William A. Pickett
Annie Moore Smith
Larry Douglass Stepp
Ethel M. Whitfield
James E. Whitefield
Nellie E. Williams

DUPLIN COUNTY AFRICAN AMERICAN AMERICAN CEMETERIES

Sam Miller Cemetery
Warsaw, North Carolina

Lela M. Ammons
Johnnie R. Artis Sr.
Luther Beatty
Robert Lee Beatty
James A. Bell
Gwendolyn E. Bell
Andrew Roy Best
Cornelia Best
Rev. James Arthur Best
James Norman Best
Robert Lee Best
Sidney Mae Beatty
Anthony G. Blackmon
Mildred S. Blue
Raymond Boone
Annie Lucille Bouyer
Annie Bell Bowden
Mary Inez Bowden
Adelle A. Branch
Rev. Matthew Stewart Branch
Oscar Branch
Julie Brewington
Lillie Smith Brewington
Teneshaia T. Brewington
Tommie Lee Brewington
Mary Louise Bronson
Michael Bronson
Louis Carol
Willie James Carroll
Everett J. Cooper
Lisa Smith Cooper
Albert Dixon
Odell Dixon
Inez H. Faison
Glen Faison
Leorns Faison
Mildred Usher Faison
Eva Beulah Frederick
Lottie C. Gooding
Mary J. Kornegay
Rudolph Kornegy
William A. Kornegay
Mildred Charles Hall
Mary Beulah Hand
Otis Hardy
Dana McDuffie Harvey
Jimmy Lee Harvey Jr.
Nellie Hicks
Robert Hicks
Dixie Louise Hines
Charles Hodges
Donald Avon Hodges
Freddie James Hodges
Katie Miller Hodges
Lloyd Berry Hodges
Mattie M. Hodges
Margie Hodges
Odell Elizabeth Hodges
Willie E. Hodges
Theodore Holmes
Cleora Williams Jones
Corrine Jones
James K. Jones
Ernest Lamb
Zuella Lamb
Frances Mae Hill Livingston
Laurence Livingston
Edna D. Lowe
Henry E. Lowe
Julie H. Lowe
Oshenia S. A. Lowe
Dorothy L. Martin

DUPLIN COUNTY AFRICAN AMERICAN AMERICAN CEMETERIES

Sam Miller Cemetery
Warsaw, North Carolina

Earl Austin Martin Maye
George A. Maye
Carrie Mae Martin
Henry Martin
Henry L. Martin III
Henry L. Martin Jr.
James Leonard Martin
Lena Martin
Odessa C. Martin
Owen Bryant Martin
William James Martin
Pearl Austin Martin Maye
Mary Mageline McDuffie
Earlene Darden Melvin
John Hiram McIver
Abbie Miller
Essie Miller
Daniel Harold Miller
William Henry Miller
James Sam Miller
Wayne E. Miller
Evelyn W. Moore
William Henry Moore
Victor Bernard Moore Sr.
Thurman Andrew Ricks
James Otis Sampson Jr.
Tina Sampson
Dancy C. Smith
Rev. Jimmy Smith
Leroy Smith
Nathan Bryant Smith
Nathan Smith
Theron M. Smith
Jerimiah Stokes
Helen Roten Synder
Bud Taylor
Robert Lee Thomas Jr.
Annie Neacy Chestnut Thompson
John Robert Thompson
Fanny Jimenez Torres
Chaz R. Moni Troublefield
Tenner Vann
Joseph C. Waters
Annie J. Allen Wells
Rev. Sumler V. Wells
Narcissus Wiggins
Dorothy E. Williams
Essie Mae Whitehead Williams
Eva W. Williams
Rev. George Dudley Williams Jr.
Garland Grant Williams
George Henry Williams
Lina Christine Smith Williams
McCoy Williams
Richard Williams
Roosevelt Williams
William M. Williams
Stephan A. Winsom
Dorothy G. Wilson
Herman Wilson
James Henry Wilson
Willie Mae Williams Wilson

DUPLIN COUNTY AFRICAN AMERICAN AMERICAN CEMETERIES

Friendship Baptist Church Cemetery
Rosehill, North Carolina

James C. Anderson
Narcisa Williams Anderson
SSGT. Herbert John Artis
Mary Lossie Barnhill
Diamond Bennett
Inez Evans Bright
Annie L. Brown
Christopher Brown
Clara Mae Brown
Johnnie Mack Brown
Juanita Brown
Mary Lue Brown
Sylvester Brown Jr.
Sylvester Brown Sr.
Tracy Renee Brown
Virginia Caroline Brown
Dorothy S. Bryant
Addie W. Butler
Paul D. Butler
Patricia Carlton
Wallace Carlton
Andrew Jackson Carr
Garlie Chasten
Della Ann Faison Chestnut
Jannatha Rogers Cromity
Dennis Crumpler
Eliza Mollie Crumpler
Elliott Crumpler
Junius M. Crumpler
Mary Belle Devane Crumpler
Oleta L. Crumpler
Vernia Crumpler
Dorothy Mae Crumpler-Graham
Geraldine Cummings
William L. Cummings
William Thomas Davis
Essie Newkirk Devane
Maggie Ruth Dixon
David Evans
Mary Butler Stringfield Evans
James Faison
Rena Faison
Edna Faison Fisher
Roy R. Fisher
Sallie M. Fryer
Katherine Stallings Green
Jason D. Jackson
Mary H. Jacobs
Thomas James Jacobs
Garfield D. Johnson
Ida Mary Johnson
Luda Johnson
Lucious Jones
Jeremiah Kenan
Latonia Kay Kenan
Ernest D. Kenan
Mary L. Matthews King
Gabrielle Leach
Maddison Faith Leach
Noel Leach
Annie Ruth Anderson Mathis
Arthur Lee Mathis
Cleveland Mathis
Fisher Wells Mathis
Hazel E. Mathis
James McKinley Mathis
Jannie B. Mathis
John Robert Mathis
levy James Mathis
Nealie Mathis
Oscar Thomas Mathis
Rufus Carriel Mathis
Shelby Ann Mathis
Josephone McGilliam
Hazel W. Melvin
Elizabeth Merritt

DUPLIN COUNTY AFRICAN AMERICAN AMERICAN CEMETERIES

Friendship Baptist Church Cemetery
Rosehill, North Carolina

Wendy Milton
Vernon Lee Mitchell
Minnie M. Mott
Minnie M. Mott
Sarah Lee Murphy
Stanley Murphy
Anna Lalestine Mosley Newkirk
Jeremiah Newkirk Sr.
Mary Elizabeth Johnson-Newkirk
Timothy R. Newkirk
David Paterson
James A. Peterson
Alice Juanita Picket
Benjamin Johnson Pickett
Alice Juanita Pickett
Malik Demont Pollock
Sarah Frances Rhodie Pollock
Bryan Keith Rhodes
Dewitt Rhodes
Dorothy M. Rhodes
Eva Mae Evans Rhodes
Lloyd Ashley Rhodes
Lloyd J. Rhodes
Luther D. Rhodes
Maurice Rhodes

Pamela Ann Rhodes
Willie F. Rhodes
King Soloman Rhodie
Micheal Wayne Rhodie
Effie B. Robinson
Garry Robinson
Larry Robinson
Lester Shaw Sr.
Mary A. William Shaw
Ellen Stringfield Spearman
Charles Edward Stallings
Glendale Stallings
James Raeford Stallings
Mary Bell Mathis Stallings
Christine Stringfield
Henry Stringfield
Henry Thompson
William F. Thompson
Rosetta Newkirk Tillery
Dianne Johnson Twitty
George Twitty
George Twitty
Willis Benson Underwood

Cardell Wallace
Alice Carroll Wells
Vera Stringfield
Evans-Wells
Hattie B. West
Mary J. West
Berta Williams
Chakita A. Williams
Ellen S. William
J. L. Williams
James F. Williams
James T. Williams
Jannie Gregory William
Joe Luther Williams
john Ander Williams
Lottie V. Williams
Luther Graham Williams
Willie Albert Williams
Fontella S. Wilson
Latricia Katrice Wilson
Roosevelt Wilson
Sheila Wilson
William M. Wilson
Charlie M. Wilson
Charlie Young
Svannah P. Young

DUPLIN COUNTY AFRICAN AMERICAN AMERICAN CEMETERIES
Farrior Cemetery
Island Creek Township, North Carolina

Pearlie Austin
Lillie Mae Baysden
Estellea Bryant
Hattie W. Burgess
Julius D. Burgess
Dorothy L. Chasten
Lott Chasten
Mary Kelly Chasten
Darlean Young Cole
Essie Mae Farrior Days
A. J. Dixon
Arthur Dock Dixon
Charlie Mae Jarman Dixon
Hayes Dixon
James E. Dixon
Marie F. Dixon
Maydell Farrior Dixon
Roland Dixon
Rose Emma Farrior Dixon
Rosa L. Everett
Albert H. Farrior
Albert L. Farrior
Alexander Evander Farrior
Alice Pearl Farrior
Annie O. Farrior
Conovia Farrior
Coy Farrior
Daniel Hosea Farrior
Dock D. Farrior
Douglass Eugene Farrior
Eddie D. Farrior
Edeo Farrior
Eller Farrior
Estella Farrior
Eva Chasten Farrior
Isaac James Farrior
James Rufus Farrior
John William Farrior
Kenneth Farrior
Lacy Jane Brown Farrior
Lillian L. Farrior
Lora H. Farrior
Maggie Emma McArthur Farrior
Maiden Earl Farrior
Marcus L. Farrior
Mary Ann Farrior
Nellie Farrior
Norman Farrior
Percy Farrior
Ruth M. Farrior
Sarha W. Farrior
Tommie Ward Farrior
Willie Davis Farrior
Alice Marie Furlow
George W. Furlow II
Mary Furlow
Roosevelt Furlow
Pauline F. Graham
Millie D. Green
Dan D. Herring
Dolly A. Farrior Herring
Polly J. Herring
Wilbert E. herring
Ella Mae Hill
Joe Lewis Hill
Josie Lee Hill
Andrew James
Geraldine H. James
L. Weeks James
Rachel Bell James
Lillie B. James
Charles H. Kenan Jr.
Mary Farrior Kenan
Priscilla Farrior Kenan
Charlie Kenan
John Lanier

DUPLIN COUNTY AFRICAN AMERICAN AMERICAN CEMETERIES

Carr Cemetery
Island Creek Township, North Carolina

Rachel Lanier
William Lanier
Fred Lak
M. Roxie Leak
Emma F. Luck
James O. Matthews
Doshie F. McDonald
Corey Jermaine Moore
Robert Murray
William J. Murray
Willie F. Newkirk
Mensah Gyasi Oluyemi
Carolyn H. Owens
Robert James Perkins
Virginia Farrior Perkins
Douglass Paul Price
Rosalind Anita Quarterman
Ellouise D. Reese
Kirby L. Rochelle
Maggie F. Rochelle
Sam Rochelle
Mary R. Williams
Samuel Witherspoon
Jimmie L. Wooten
George Young
Maggie Pearl Farrior Young

DUPLIN COUNTY AFRICAN AMERICAN AMERICAN CEMETERIES

Dudley Smith Cemetery
Kenansville, North Carolina

Ida C. Evans
Willie Joyce Garner
Clint Smith
Dennis Ray Smith
Doris Smith
Doy Smith Smith
Dudley Smith
Edward Junior Smith
Joe Nathan Smith
Joseph Hill Smith
Lawton C. Smith

Martha Ellen Outlaw Smith
Moses Smith
Percella Catherine Williams Smith
Percy Smith
Ralph F. Smith
Rayford Smith
Sylvia Darden Smith
Sylvia Diane Smith
Versale Everett Smith
Willie L. Smith
Kelvin Lionell Webb

DUPLIN COUNTY AFRICAN AMERICAN AMERICAN CEMETERIES

Cobb Cemetery
Faison, North Carolina

Eddie E. Adams
James Henry Adams
Jesse W. Adams
Ophelia Frances Crowe Adams
Leslie Lee Allen
Annie E. Armwood
Charles Armwood
Evelyn B. Armwood
Gertie Lee Armwood
J. Christopher Armwood
Kilby Armwood
Leonard Armwood
Lillie Armwood
Margaret Armwood
Matthew Armwood
Wasby Armwood
Wiley J. Armwood
Jaylin Antonia Artis
JessieArtis
Maria Nanette Artis
Betty Barksdale Ashford
Booker T. Ashford
Charles Ashford
Effie Jane Ashford
John H. Ashford
Maggie Ashford
Pitt Ashford
Robert Ashford
William Lloyd Ashford
Mattie B. Avery
William Avery
Alberta Simmons Aycock
Alford Aycock
Candis B. Aycock
Jessie T. Aycock
john E. Aycock
Rev. Marion Aycock Sr.
Peggy Jean Aycock
Eric Todd Badger
Keith Darnell Badger
Bertha Baggett
Ira Baggett
Nathan Baggett
Willa J. Baggett
Winston Baggett
Fred A. Barksdale
Jessie Lee Barksdale
Leanmon Barksdale
Lillie Mae Faison Barksdale
Walter Barksdale
O'Berry Beaman
Cornell Becton
Jenkie H. Becton
Delois G. Bell
Dorcus Bell
Eilher Freeman Bell
Freddie Bell
Furnie David Bell
Howard Tauissant Bell
Jessie David Bell
Jessie L. Bell
Maggie Darden Bell
Mary Darden Bell
Minnie Taylor Bell
Nellie A. Bell
Nolan Arcadas Bell

229

DUPLIN COUNTY AFRICAN AMERICAN AMERICAN CEMETERIES

Cobb Cemetery
Faison, North Carolina

Ranso H. Bell
Spec Reginald Conrad Bell
Sallie Fryar Bell
Shirley N. Bell
William L. Bell
Bunyan Benjamin
Charlie Benjamin
Clarence Benjamin
Hester Brinson Benjamin
Leroy Benjamin
Mildred Benjamin
Samuel Benjamin
Joe R. Bennett
Josephine Hand Bennett
Easter Best
Howard Best
Doan James Blount
Jessie Faison Blount
Letha Lamb Blount
Robert Aaron Blount
Leon Blue

Charlotte Bowden
David A. Bowden
John R. Bowden
Helen H. Boyette
William Boyette
Janice F. Boyette-Ludwig
Annie M. Branch
Annie Marie Brewington
Elizabeth Brewington
Hannah W. Brewing
Julius B. Brewington
Leary D. Brewington
Lillie Brewington
Lloyd Brewington Jr.
Lucy E. Brewington
Rose B. Brewington
Thomas F. Brewington
Lucille Stanford Brewington
Melvin Bridges
Anna Marie Simmons Bright
Lucy Mae Bright Bristow

Alfred Broadhurst
Cornelius Brown
Gracie L. Brown
Mary McClamb Brown
George Brunson
Gloria Brunson
Gregory Devone Bronson
Diane B. Bryant
Rufus Bunting
Allie Butler
Alonzo Butler
Ella Lee Butler
George Hebert Butler
Emma L. Carlton
Mary Lou Smith Prince Carlton
Samuel Preston Carlton
Lonnie P. Carr
Beulah Mae Craddock-Carrence
Litha Mae Aycock Cates
Charles Chalmers
Mary Jane Thompson Chalmers

DUPLIN COUNTY AFRICAN AMERICAN AMERICAN CEMETERIES

Cobb Cemetery
Faison, North Carolina

Carthel Cobb
Charlie Cobb
Daisy Belle Sutton Cobb
Harvey J. Cobb Sr.
Lila M. Cobb
Mary W. Cobb
Matthew Cobb
Matthew James Cobb
Sula M. Cobb
William Arthur Cobb
Mary W. Cobbs
Winston Cobbs
Dixie Mae Contry
Charlie Conyus
John C. Cox
Maggie D. Cox
Flonza Craddock
Hattie Jane Craddock
Velonzo Craddock
William E. Craddock
Willie R. Craddock
Roland C. Crawford
Charles C. Crawford
Charles James Darden
Craig L. Darden
Helen Darden
Jesse L. Darden
Willie Arthur Darden
Willie David Darden
Bee W. Dent
Carrie M. Dent
Flora S. Dent
Harry Dent
Jimmie S. Dent
Florence Draughon
Bobby G. Edwards
John Edwards
Josephine Edwards
Kendrick Lamont Edwards
Maryland Edwards Jr.
Minnie Ruth Elliott
Estve Ermilus
Carrie Lee Everett
Eva Exumn
Oscar Ezzell
Alice Ruth Thompson Faison
Almira Lofton Faison
Annie Pearl Smith Faison
Clarence Faison
Cressul Faison
Darrell Edward Faison
Dilsey Southerland Faison
Dorothy Faison
Eddie E. Faison Jr.
Ernestine Faison
Hannah Ashford Faison
Harry W. Faison
Hazel Faison
Howard G. Faison
Hubert E. Faison
Rev. I. W. Faison
Isaac James Faison
Isham Faison

DUPLIN COUNTY AFRICAN AMERICAN AMERICAN CEMETERIES

Cobb Cemetery
Faison, North Carolina

James Elliott Faison Sr.
Janie B. Faison
Joyce Waters Faison
Julia A. Faison
Kenneth Ray Faison
Lacy R. Faison
Lillie Mae Faison
Malcolm D. Faison
Martha Stevens Faison
Mary Margniana Faison
Matthew Lee Faison
Melva Beamon Faison
Michael Devon Faison
Napoleon Faison Jr.
Napoleon Faison Sr.
Odell H. Faison
Phylander Faison
Ronnie Faison
Sadie Bell Hobbs Faison
Sadie E. Faison

Samuel E. Faison
Thomas Faison
Tydmon Faison
Wilbert Faison
William Faison
Willie A Faison
Willie R. Faison
Wilma Joyce Faison
Mary Virginia Darden Flanagan
Doris Odessa Brewington Flanagan
Garfield Flanagan Jr.
Infant Boy Fogelman
Alonza Foy
Frances Fryar
Hiawatha Fryar
Peter Fryar
Peter D. Fryar
Rose Bell Smith Fryar
Samuel Fryar Sr.
Elouise Faison Fryer

Annie Martha Branch Garner
Rev. Arthur Garner
Lillie Belle Garner
Noah George Garris
Bessie George
Evandus V. George
Inetta William George
Larry Earl George
Lucile Hicks George
Maurice P. George
Nathaniel George Sr.
Noah George
Noah C. George
Reatha Bell Fryar George
Sampson George
Samuel L. George
Craig Gillard Jr.
Frances Goodman
Hubert Goodman
James Atlas Goodman

DUPLIN COUNTY AFRICAN AMERICAN AMERICAN CEMETERIES

Cobb Cemetery
Faison, North Carolina

Juanita Williams Goodman
Prycilla D. Grandy
Annie H. Green
Annie Greene
April M. Hall
Addie L. Hargrove
Annie H. Green
Annie Greene
April M. Hall
Addie L. Hargrove
Hattie R. Hargrove
Hosea Hargrove
Jerome Hargrove
Jim W. Hargrove
Leslie E. Hargrove
Mary L. Hargrove
Percy Hargrove
Ralph Hargrove
Susan J. Hargrove
Walter A. Hargrove

Delois McDuffie Harper
Edna Earl Latter Harper
James Earl Harper
James Henry Harper Sr.
Jim Davis Harper Sr.
Jimmy Lee Harper
Lola Lucille Smith Harper
Ruth A. Harper
Wilden Harper Sr.
Annie Mae Williams Harrell
Mary W. Harrell
William I. Harrell
Hattie Harrington
Baby Harvey
Mary Linda Harvey
Mary L. Adams Hayden
Florence V. Hemingway
Jeremiah Hemingway
Billie Sunday Herring
Alma T. Hick

Kinnon Hicks
Lucille Hicks
Samuel M. Hicks
Jannie B. Highsmith
Barbara Ann Hill
Catherine Louise Hill
Curtis Lee Hill
Delia Blount Hill
Edwin Roscoe Hill
Emma Clyde Hill
Ervin Hill Jr.
Harry L. Hill Sr.
Juanita Bryant Hill
Rev. Julius Hill
Katie E. Hill
Kenneth Antonio Hill
Ola Mae Hill
Robert Lee Hill
Catherine Hobbs
Doretha Hobbs

DUPLIN COUNTY AFRICAN AMERICAN AMERICAN CEMETERIES

Cobb Cemetery
Faison, North Carolina

Flonnie Hobbs
John C. Hobbs
Linwood Earl Hobbs
Mary Jane Hobbs
Nancy Catherine Hobbs
Rudolph Hobbs
Weldon Turner Hobbs
Willie Mae Hobbs
Albert Hodges
Caroline Hicks Hodges
Henry Hodges
Lanie Hodges
William L. Holmes
Elizabeth Maricia Cobb Horne
Hebert Houston
Lorenzo W. Howard
William M. Howard II
Jennifer P. Howell
Julia S. Howell
Demetrius Devon Hudson

Martha Hussey
Dock Ireland
Maggie E. Ireland
William Jackson
Jesse James
Nyshawn Nathaniel Jasso
Annie O. Johnson
Johnnie Lee Johnson
Novella Johnson
Betty M. Jones
Blanche B. Jones
David Jones
Velma Gray Bland Jones
Ada Elizabeth Joyner
Jonathan Joyner
Louis Henry Joyner
Katherine Kelly
Robert Kelly
Drummont E. King
Kenneth Debois King

Annie R. Kornegay
Kenneth Aaron Kornegay
Macon R. Kornegay
Andrew T. Leach
Betsy F. Leach
James H, Leach
James H. Leach Jr.
Savannah Jane Barksdale Leach
Stephen Robert Leach
Armatha G. Leas
Frances Helen Lee Bell
Rev. Joe Lee
Luevater Lee
Kenneth L. Leonard
J. Antwan Lewis
Robert Lewis Sr.
Sarah Lewis
George Ralph Little Jr.
Willie Loftin
Kathleen J. Lofton

DUPLIN COUNTY AFRICAN AMERICAN AMERICAN CEMETERIES

Cobb Cemetery
Faison, North Carolina

Nellie Bringht Marshall
Angela Massey
Clarence Mathis
Lenora C. Mathis
Levie Mathis
Mary Mathis
Minnie C. Mathis
William H, Mathis
Hosea Matthew Sr.
Pennie A. Matthews
William Earl McClarin
Dr. Grace S. McDonald
Latash Yolanda Denee McDuffie
Lester Thomas McDuffie Sr.
Robert Earl McDufee
Sallie Wright McDuffie
Wade McDuffie
Catherine McKiethan
Helen McKiethan
Robert McKiethan
Johnnie McKinney
Rev. Omelia G. McKinney
Eliza Royal McLamb
Janie Delois McLeod
Edward McLean Jr.
Adell McNair
Amelia Faison M<elvin
Johnnie Lee Middleton
Curtis H. Mimms
Charlie Bryant Mitchell
Rev. Elaine Mitchell
Lillie Belle James Mitchell
Bernice Moore
Carrie J. Moore
Faison Thomas Moore
Gertrude Baggett Moore
Gloria Jean Whitfield
Handson O. Moore
Hattie T. Moore
Kenneth Ray Moore
Lizzie Bryant Moore
Louise T. Moore
Percy Moore
Roberta Moore
Thomas Earl Moore
Vicky M. Moore
Alberta B. Morrisey
Carrie Jean Morrisey
Linda Morrisey
Nettie Bright Morrisey
William M. Morrisey
Frank Hart Murray
Lucille Cole Newkirk
Lucius Newkirk
Mary Lily Newkirk
Rufus Newkirk
Della Jane Warren Newsome
Andra Marcble Oates
Bernice H. Oakes
Claretha S. Oates
Curtis E. Oates
Donald Ray Oates
Eddie Oates
Henry Oates Jr.
James Henry Oates
Jessie J. Oates
Lounmis H. Oates

DUPLIN COUNTY AFRICAN AMERICAN AMERICAN CEMETERIES

Cobb Cemetery
Faison, North Carolina

Richard L. Oates
Robert E. Oates
Thamitchel Faison Oates
Vennie Ree Ashford Oates
Beatrice Oats
John Ezekiel Oats
Pearlie L. Oats
Theodore Owens
Charlie F. Parker
Henry L. Parker
James Parker
Katie A. Parker
Lillie E. Parker
Luther C. Parker
Maggie J. Parker
Richard M. Parker
Shirley Jean Parker
Roberta Benjamin Patterson
Maxine Tann Peacock
Henry F. People
Kenneth E. Peoples
Reaths Peoples
Christopher Columbus Philyaw
Lillie Bell Smith Philyaw

Martha V. Powell
Theodore Powell
Menzo Price
Lubertha B. Pride
Tammoris N. Raynor
Nettie A. Ried
Dr. Lemuel R. Revels
Clarice Robison
Eudell Ross
Ivey Donnell Royal
Ivey Royal
Betty Louise Bright Russell
Charles Sampson
Charlie Sampson
Francis S. Sampson
Mary Sampson
William Sampson
Benjamin Samuel
John Needham Sanders Jr.
Maylon Hobbs Sanders
Vera S. Scott
Bobby Lee Seaberry Jr.

Beadie L. Shambly
Henry Shaw
Mabel Shaw
Ivey Lee Sherrod
Marion Lamont Sherrod
Edward Shine
Annette Simmons
Betty T. Simmons
James Bobby Simmons
Johnnie B. Simmons
Lula Simmons
Lwander Simmons
Mary E. Simmons
Pelham Simmons
Quessie Simmons
Rufus M. Simmons Sr.
Solomon Simmons
Tremayne L. Simmons Jr.
Vera I. Simmons
Carl L. Simpson
Lillian Singleton
Terry L. Singleton
Isham F. Slocumb Jr.
Minnie Bryant Slocumb

DUPLIN COUNTY AFRICAN AMERICAN AMERICAN CEMETERIES

Cobb Cemetery
Faison, North Carolina

Beatrice Smith
Bobby Gene Smith
Charles Autry Smith
Clayton Kenneth Smith
Elizabeth Smith
Elnora Smith
Emeline Giles Smith
Frances Bell smith
Georgia M. Smith
James Franklin Smith
James Walter Smith
Jessie Lee Smith
Leroy L. Smith
Leslie David Smith
Lessie Smith
Lessie J. Smith
Lucille B. Smith
Nursey M. Smith
Rosa Mae Swinson Smith
Sadie B. Smith
Sallie T. Smith
Rev. Scipio Smith
Will Smith
Silphia Swinson Smith
Adreian Boyd Solomon
Angeline McDuffie Starkie
Algeon Stevens
Annie Belle Hodges Stevens
Arathra Stevens
Bernice Stevens
Bessie Jolyn Stevens
Blanch Stevens
Charlie Russelle Rogers Stevens
Davis E. Stevens
Essie Pearl Stevens
Geneva Stevens
Gordan Stevens
Jessie Broadhurst Stevens
Jessie Bell Broadhurst Stevens
John Stevens
Johnnie Stevens
Leary Stevens
Lillie Stevens
Lonnie Stevens
Mable A. Stevens
Mary Stevens
Matthews Stevens
Matthews Lee Stevens Sr.
Maxine Kelly Stevens
McClure Stevens
Melissa Stevens
Morris M. Stevens
Moses Auson Junior Stevens
Preston Squire Stevens Sr.
Ray Stevens
Reginald Stevens
Tabitha Jane Ashford Stevens
Thomas L. Stevens
Tobitha Stevens
William Arthur Ashford Stevens
Willie L. Stevens
Janie Mae Sutton
Janie Mae Sutton
Willard Floyd Sutton
Emanuel Swinson
Louise William Swinson
Robert Swinson
Sallie Jones Swinson
Samuel Swinson
Bessie M. Tann

DUPLIN COUNTY AFRICAN AMERICAN AMERICAN CEMETERIES

Cobb Cemetery
Faison, North Carolina

Daisy P. Tann
Ernest Tann
Hezekiah Tann
Jeremiah Henry Tann
Jesse Lee Tann
Joe Isaac Tann
Johnny B. Tann
Levie Tann
Louise Moore Tann
Mary Lee Tann
Matthew Richard Tann
Mattie M. Tann
Pauline King Tann
Tyron Tann
Vinnie B. Tann
Kynmora Tatchyona Tatum
Crawford W. Taylor
Ella Jane Taylor
Frank Taylor Sr.
Gary Taylor
Deacon Gary Taylor
James Taylor Jr.
John Neil Taylor
Mary Elizabeth Taylor
Willis James Taylor
Rev. Alonzo Fuller Thompson
Bertha J. Thompson
Charles Glasco Thompson
Claressie Thompson
Cora Thompson
Delton Oberry Thompson
Rev. Edgar O. Thompson
Edwin Morris Thompson
Edwin S. Thompson
Frankie Thompson
Fred Thompson
Georgia Faison Thompson
James M. Thompson
Julius Cornelius Thompson Sr.
Julius Edward Thompson
Katie C. Hampton Thompson
Madie Bea Sanders Thompson
Maggie Delia Faison Thompson
Margie Lewis Thompson
Marion D. thompson
Mary Jodie Faison Thompson
Mordecai Weldon Thompson Sr.
Nina S. Thompson
Orlando B. Thompson
Robert J. Thompson
Roscoe Thompson
Scottie B. Thompson
Thomas Luther Thompson
Lula C. Tripp
Elnora Smith Troublefield
Johnnie Lee Troublefield
Moses Troublefield
Lena Marie Bright Vann
Ronnie Vann
Percy Clifton Wallace
Annie Rebecca Smith Ward
Laura Brunson Ware
Annie M. Warren
Bessie Warren
Gladys Warren
James Doll Warren
Aaron Waters Sr.
Henry J. Waters
James H. Waters
Lillie B. Waters

DUPLIN COUNTY AFRICAN AMERICAN AMERICAN CEMETERIES

Cobb Cemetery
Faison, North Carolina

Phillip Watkins
David Weeks
Eva M. Weeks
James Egbert Weeks
Josephine Hargrove Weeks
Lela K. Weeks
Matthew D. Weeks
Mattie S. Weeks
Pelvis Weeks
Katie S. Wells
Alberta Royal West
Eugene West
Addie Lee Williams
Artie R. Williams
Bennie Russell Williams
Donald L. Williams
Evelyn Grace Williams
Hazel Craddock Williams
Leedell Williams
Lucy Fannie Williams
Mary K. Williams
Robert Williams
William H. Williams
Paul Noel Wilson
Viola P. Winston
James L. Wolfe
Martha Wolfe
Charles D. Wooten
Bonnie Brewington Wright
Eliza Jane Vann Wright
Jessie D. Wright
Patrice O. Wright

DUPLIN COUNTY AFRICAN AMERICAN AMERICAN CEMETERIES
Rose Hill Funeral Home Cemetery
Rose Hill, North Carolina

Hattie J. Alderman
William McDonald Alderman
Anthony C. Alexander Jr.
Herman Allen
Mable Louise Allen
Rudolph Allen
Adalberto Araujo
Emilio Arellano
Roosevelt Arnold
Kelvin T. Artis
Tony Lee Artis
Willie Edward Artis
Jesus Antonio Avila
Alvon Bernard Bailey
Garrick D. Bannerman
Gwen McMillian Bannerman
Kenneth Dale Bannerman
Lucy M. Barber
Mary Effie Rogers Barnes
Joe Lee Barnes
Nachito Bartolo
James E. Basden
Deloris Delreo Batts

Charlie E. Bethea
Ernest Hartzel Bethea Sr.
Frank Bethea Jr.
Frank Pearsall Bethea
Mary Perasall Bethea
Mildred Bethea
William D. Bethea
Maggie L. Usher Bland
Felix H. Bland
Mable M. Branch
Hattie Frances Jordan Brice
Willie Frances Brice
Ernest Cleveland Bright
Katie M. Brimage
Ada Elizabeth Glaspie Brinson
John Thomas Brinson
Julia Ann Brinson
Robert Louis Brinson
Willie Brinson
Willie Raymond Brinson
Coy Brown
Florence Henry Brown

Lillian Bryant Brown
Marion Earl Brown
William Brown
Charlie R. Bryant Jr.
Jessie Mae Pearsall Bryant
Joseph S. Bryant
Pollie W. Bryant
Vistella Lee Gibbs Bryant
Willie L. Bryant
Annie N. Bryd
Minnie Cherry Byrd
Jonathan R. Cano
Ayrie Carlton
Catherine W. Carlton
Clarence Edward Carlton
Ervin Lee Carlton
Henry Thomas Carlton
James Franklin Carlton
James Henry Carlton
James Wilson Carlton
Maggie R. Carlton
Mary Lou Lamb Carlton
Mary S. Carlton
Sylvester Carlton Sr.

DUPLIN COUNTY AFRICAN AMERICAN AMERICAN CEMETERIES

Rose Hill Funeral Home Cemetery
Rose Hill, north Carolina

Vance Carlton
Addie Morris Carroll
Addie Morris Carroll Sr.
Albert Carroll
Booker T. Carroll
Sudie M. Carroll
David Andrew Carroll
Eddie Lee Carter
Ronnie Carter
Robert Lee Carter
Mildred Westbrook Cherry
Anderson Jermaine Chester
Christopher Donta Clibbons
Apostle Washington Coleman Jr.
Dorothy Elizabeth Merritt-Comergys Parker
Fostina Lisane Cooper
Maggie L. Cooper
Annie Rogers Corbett
Ella A. Coston
Estella Gertrude Bennerman Coston
Robert Coston
Telpha Coston
Thomas Mckinley Coston
James Henry Cromity
James Davis
Richard Davis
Richard L. Davis Jr.
Roland L. Davis jr.
Roland Lee Davis
Rudolph Davis
Robert L. DeVone Sr.
Cleveland Dixon
Jimmy Lee Dixon
Junices L. Dixon
Lillie G. Dixon
Maggie Ruth Dixon
Norwood Dixon
Rita S. Dixon
Arthur Dobson
Lonnie Bryant Dobson
Fannie B. Dove
James Henry Dove Jr.
John E. Dudley
Frazier C. Duran
Henry M. Ellis
Willia A. Fant
George Farmer
Adolphus Farrior
Clarence Farrior
Claudie Odell Farrior Jr.
George Faulk
Michael Rennie Faulk
Lorraine N. Faylor
Rev. Diamond Council Fennell
Jannie H. Fennell
Leroy Fennell
Mary Jane Simmons Fennell
Ralph Fennell
Beulah M. Fields
Geneva J. Fredericks
Isaac Frederick
King David Frederick
Matthew Frederick Sr.
Moses David Frederick
Patricia A. Frederick
Rena Mae Nicherson Frederick

DUPLIN COUNTY AFRICAN AMERICAN AMERICAN CEMETERIES

Rose Hill Funeral Home Cemetery
Rose Hill, north Carolina

Ruth Dixon Frederick
F. Nathaniel Furlow
Josh E. Fussell
Mary Gatling
Robert R. Gatling
Carrie B. Gause
George Geronimo Gay
Adell Robinson Gibbs
Henry Alex Gibbs
Lucy Mae Boney Gibbs
William Thomas Gillespie
Mary J. Glaspie
Rufus Glaspie
Walter L. Glaspie
William T. Glaspie
Lashawn M. Godwin
Fancy H. Graham
Elnora D. Gray
Jessie C. Hall
Norman Fairey Hall
Julius Hardin
james Walter Hatcher

Leroy Hatcher
Vara Lee Fennell Hatcher
Flora Henry
James D. Henry
Margater D. Herny
Ronald D. Henry
Willie D. Henry
Katie Herring
Rev. Kenneth Leroy Herring
Daisy B. Highsmith
Paulette Kornegay Hill
William G. Hodges
Annie Holmes
Callie Holmes
Catherine Holmes
Mildred Holmes
Walter Holmes
Albert Huguina

Irene C. Huguina
Joyce Ann James
Ollen James
Domese Jeantal
William Henry Johnson
Alexander Jones
Floretta Jane Wiliams Jones
Oscar Thomas Jones
James Daniel kea
Wilma Lee Kea
Donald Ray Kenan
LaVoice Carr Keana
Retha Mae Witherspoon Kean
Willie Bobbie Kenan
William Henry Kenan
Baby Boy Knickerson
Brutus Kornegay
Eva Kornegay
Henry Kornegay
Jessie Kornegay
Daisy Bell Pearsall Lamb
Redtha W. Lanier

DUPLIN COUNTY AFRICAN AMERICAN AMERICAN CEMETERIES

Rose Hill Funeral Home Cemetery
Rose Hill, North Carolina

Betty Jean Clibbons Lee
John H. Lee
Johnnie Mae Lee
Timothy Wesley Lewis
Martha L. London
Herbert L. Marshall Jr.
Frances Beaty Mathis
James F. Mathis
Ronnie McClide
Thelma McCoy
Cathy L. Mcfadden
Ladell McFadden
Dallas McKinney
Spec Dallas Ervin McKinny Jr.
Baby McKiver
Carley McMillan
Dwight McMillian
Jay H. McMilian
Jhetong Eduardo Merino
James Merriman
Charles Merritt

James Mettitt
James W. Merritt
Lillie W. Merritt
Sadie L. Merritt
Alberta S. Middleton
Ethel P. Middleton
Willie Anderson Middleton
Stevie C. Miller
Veronia Mae Kenan Miller
Mary A. Mitchell
Levy James Monroe
Irene Andrews Montgomery
Malachi Montgomery
Annie Jane Lamb Moore
Bessie S. Moore
Erzaline W. Moore
Lillian Goldie Houston Moore
Lindsey W. Moore
Lloyd T. Moore

Lloyd Tolento Moore
Matthew Moore
Nettie R. Moore
Phebie M. Moore
William Moore
Willie L. Moore
Maquenly A. Moradel
Mary C. Munson
Donquella Murphy
Earl David Murphy
Ella Ray Beatty Murphy
Jessie Mae Miller Murphy
Norman D. Murphy
Oliver T. Murphy
Richard McCoy Murphy
Ruby W. Murphy
Stanley Leon Murphy
Thelmas Fennel Murphy
Winfred Avery Murphy
Beverly Murphy-Parrott
Carolyn Patricia Murray

DUPLIN COUNTY AFRICAN AMERICAN AMERICAN CEMETERIES

Rose Hill Funeral Home Cemetery
Rose Hill, North Carolina

Helen Elizabeth Murray
Lula Mae Murray
Virgie L. Murray
Fred R. Neil
Sadie A. Neil
Anner B. Newkirk
Essex Claude Newkirk
Gertrude Coston
Hattie Jane Carlton Newkirk
Ida Bell Newkirk
Immis O. Newkirk
Irene C. Newkirk
James Edward Newkirk
James H,. Newkirk Sr.
John R. Newkirk
Kirk D. Newkirk
Kirk Douglass Newkirk
Vann D. Vann
Thomas W. Newton
Baby Boy Nickerson
Melissa Nicole Olivera
Dagoberta Ovando

Darlene B. Parker
Annette Pearsall
Ceymour Pearsall
Charlie W. Pearsall
Elwood Maceo Pearsall
Eugene Pearsall
Ezekial Pearsall
Henry Pearsall
Josephine Murphy Pearsall
Mamie Lee Brinson Pearsall
Margie McLean Pearsall
Martha E. Pearsall
Mary Wright Bass Pearsall
Silas Richard Pearsall
Theodore Pearsall
William Essex Pearsall
Alice Cornelia Murphy People
Ruthel Coston Pickett
Thelma Pickett
David L. Pigford

Lizzie Pearsall Pigford
Ruby Lee Pearsall Pigford
Elder Samuel D. Pigford
Clifton Pollock
James E. Pollock
Kelvin Potts
Brenda B. Powell
Carolyn D. Pryor
Aliza H. Ray
Joseph Resper
Irene B. Rhodes
Joyce Elizabeth Ricer
Mary Williams Richmond
Charlie Don Vincent Robinson Jr.
Flora C. McCallum Robison
Graham A. Robinson
Louise Pearsall Robinson
Robert B. Robinson
Alford Rogers
George Rogers
Joseph Lloyd Rogers
Lashelia F. Rogers
Isiah Sanders Sr.

DUPLIN COUNTY AFRICAN AMERICAN AMERICAN CEMETERIES

Rose Hill Funeral Home Cemetery
Rose Hill, North Carolina

Amelia Pickett Savage
Ernestine Teachy Savage
Robert Hill Savage
Pauline Pearsall Scarborough
Franklin Scott
Tommir R. Scott
Jorge Luis Serrano
Katie C. Shaw
Oscar Shaw Jr.
Georgeianne Barnes Sidberry
Zander Lee Simmons
Kathy Jean Lamb Sloan
Pearly Lee Sloan
Charles Edward Smith
James Edward Smith
Jean Carolyn Glaspie Smith
Kysheem A, Smith
Liston Smith
Mary Jane Williams Smith
McDuffie Smith
Teresa G. Smith
Elora Ambrose Southerland
Ginnie M. Southerland
James R. Southerland
Daisy L. Stallings
William C. Stallings
Elder Willie W. Stallings
Henry Stokes
Levern H. Stokes
Henderson Stroud
Victor Surita
Kenneth R. Sutton Sr.
Larry J. Swann
Willie Swann
Thaddeus Tate
Iris Torres
Haley Elena Trejo-Hernandez
Annie Viola Tyler
Edgar Tyler
Josua Tyler
Mary S. Tyler
Henry Davis usher
Marinda Beatrice Southerland Vann
James T. Wade
Annie O. Wallace
Linwood Wallace
Lizzie J. Wallace
Alexis M. Walls
Eliza Ophelia South Ward
Curtis Lamare Warren
George E. Wells
Octavie G. Wells
Bennie M. Whitehead
Willie G. Whitehead
Darnell Whitfield
James Whitfield
Rasean D. Wigley
Avery T. Williams
Charlie Henry Williams
James Avery Williams
James Robert Williams
Lissie Williams
Lucy M. Williams
Lula M. Williams
Maggie W. Williams
Retha Bell Williams
Samuel Williams Sr.
Samuel T. Williams
Terrell Williams
Artie G. Wilson
Denitia Deshun Wilson
Esther L. Wilson
Sadie M. Wilson
Willie J. Wilson

Made in the USA
Middletown, DE
25 May 2024

54685523R00146